The Prisoner
of Cell 47

by Sabrina Grossman

SOCIETY OF YOUNG INKLINGS

The Prisoner of Cell 47
Copyright © 2022 Sabrina Grossman
Requests for information should be addressed to:
Society of Young Inklings, PO Box 26914, San Jose, CA 95126.

This is a work of fiction. Unless otherwise indicated, all the names, characters, businesses, places, events and incidents in this book are either the product of the author's imagination or used in a fictitious manner. Any resemblance to actual persons, living or dead, or actual events is purely coincidental.

This manuscript was published through Society of Young Inklings' Fresh Ink imprint. Fresh Ink is an introductory publishing program for youth writers who have completed a full draft of a novel. This program introduces revision techniques which the youth author then applies to their completed draft. The views of the author are their own and do not reflect the views of Society of Young Inklings.

Cover Illustration: Keira Stolowitz
Interior Design and Layout: Kristen Schwartz
Printed in the USA
First Printing: June 2022
ISBN: 978-1-956380-18-7

To my family and friends—thank you for everything and especially for putting up with me talking about this book all the time.

Chapter 1

Artemis Hansen. That's my sister's name. She was five years old when we were taken to the Marden. Every kid like us knew that one day we would end up there, because they always find us. Always. It's been so long that I can't remember what the outside looks like. I so badly want to just step outside, and take a breath of fresh air. See the sky. Smell a flower. I was nine when Artemis and I arrived, and I'm now 14. Do the math. I haven't been outside in five years. Last year, they took her, and my mind is still haunted by the images of that day. I remember it like it was yesterday. The marching of the guards, the bitter cold that hung over the place like a blanket, the stone floor damp beneath my bare feet. Artemis was in the cell next to mine.

"Alavis, did you hear that?" she had asked me, her face appearing in the window between our cells.

"Hear what?" I had responded.

I listened closely. It was footsteps. I pulled off the black screen over the tiny window on the door to my cell, going up on my tiptoes so that I could see what was happening. The big double doors at the top of the crumbling stone staircase opened. Three tall, muscular Marden guards walked down, their faces set in a cruel glare. Their boots pounded against the ground, as they walked straight toward my cell. Or at least that's what I thought. I was terrified, and I could hear my heart beating in my chest. And then they stopped at Artemis' cell instead. One of the guards unlocked the door, and I heard screaming.

"Artemis!" I had cried out, as the guard dragged her out of the cell. "Artemis!" I yelled again, pounding on the door of my cell.

A guard appeared at my window. "Put your screen back on," she ordered.

"No."

I watched as the other two guards dragged Artemis right past my window and up the steps. She was handcuffed.

"You need to put your screen back on," the guard repeated.

I ignored her and focused my attention on the door in front of me. My hands started to heat up.

"ALAVIS!" screeched Artemis, her gray eyes filled with fear.

I concentrated as hard as I could, and the bed in my cell erupted in flames. I started to lift it up with my mind, but I stopped suddenly, watching as the metal legs of the bed began to melt. My eyes drifted over to the metal door in front of me, an idea taking root in my brain. After a moment of focusing intently, bright orange flames started to travel up the center of the door. The metal stayed perfectly intact though. Guiding the flames onto the door hinges, I held my breath hopefully. My heart nearly leapt out of my chest when the hinges started to melt. I tapped my foot anxiously against the floor, waiting for the hinges to fully melt. Luckily, it didn't take long. The second the door fell off its hinges, and then onto the floor, I rushed out. Quickly, I pushed past the guard and ran at full speed towards Artemis.

"ESCAPEE IN HALLWAY 107!" a guard had shouted.

I was so close to reaching her. And then the guards zapped

3

me, using one of the few weapons they had that worked on us magic kids. The guards took Artemis out of the room, and the door slammed shut behind them.

"NOOOOOOO!!!!!" I screamed.

The weapon had paralyzed me so I couldn't move. I couldn't get to her. I haven't seen Artemis since.

I am suddenly jolted out of my thoughts by the sound of screams. They are taking Jasmine, the girl in the cell next to mine. After they took Artemis, they started taking a person each day. Not one person has returned. You never know when you'll be taken because they take us randomly. I watch as Jasmine is taken up the stairs and out the door. After the day Artemis was taken, I was moved to a new cell. The doors to our cells were supposed to be resistant to our magic. But mine was powerful enough to break it that day. Because of this, other kids tried to use their magic to break out, but they all failed. Actually, one kid did break down the door, but he was immediately zapped. He didn't even get to the staircase. Anyway, I was moved to a special cell. I tried and tried, attempting to melt the door hinges, to burn a hole in the wall, anything really. But nothing worked. I'm not really sure if it's the new, stronger door, or if I'm just not powerful enough anymore. Maybe I was only powerful that day, when I saw them taking Artemis. Every day, I practice using my powers, so that maybe one day I'll be strong enough to break down the door again. Then, I can escape this horrid prison. I take a deep breath, sitting down on my bed, fingering the bracelet that always sits on my left wrist. Artemis gave it to me on my first birthday in the Marden. It's just a simple gray string bracelet, but it means the world to me. Aside from the fact that my little sister gave it to me, the fact that she remembered it was my birthday even after what we had gone through makes it even more precious. I remember her smiling up at me, holding out the piece of braided string.

"Happy Birthday Al," she had said, her gray eyes bright with excitement, despite the horrible place we were in.

The echo of Jasmine's screams down the hallway brings me back to the present. With a sigh, I form a fireball, throwing it at the wall of my dank, metal cell. There is a strong burning smell, but otherwise, the wall is pretty much unharmed.

"Cell 47, prisoner stand back," commands a voice.

That's me. I'm the prisoner of cell 47. But they can't be here to take me. They just took someone. They don't take two in one day! Panicking, I try to turn myself invisible, but only my arm disappears. I have been working at this for weeks, and have never gotten my whole body to disappear.

"Guards, prepare your weapons. She's stronger than the others," the voice says.

I quickly make my arm visible again. I then hear a series of clicks, and the door to my cell opens. Seven guards are standing there in the dim hallway, zapper weapons aimed at me.

"Prisoner 47, we smelled burning. Practicing your magic is not allowed, and will result in consequences. Were you practicing your magic?" one of the guards demands.

What do they expect me to say? *Oh yes, I was practicing my magic. Please, I am so excited for the consequences.*

"I was not using my magic," I lie.

I guess I should have been more careful. Usually, the burning smell is faint enough that they don't notice. Maybe this means I'm getting stronger.

"What was the burning smell?" another guard asks.

I shrug nonchalantly. "I don't smell anything burning."

"Prisoner 47, do not lie to us."

"I have a name you know," I snap, getting angry.

I hate that I'm looked at not as a person, but as a number.

"Prisoner 47—"

"You're standing pretty far away. Are you afraid of me?" I taunt, my temper getting the better of me.

"I am no—"

"That would be silly since you're the one with the weapon," I add.

"Prisoner 47, be silent or you will be paralyzed."

I may have a quick temper but I'm not stupid. I wisely decide to shut my mouth.

"REINFORCEMENTS NEEDED IN HALLWAY 123!" booms a speaker in the hallway.

"We have to leave. We won't be seeing much of you anymore after today, Prisoner 47," says one of the guards.

The seven guards head to hallway 123. My heart is racing. What did the guard mean by "we won't be seeing much of you anymore after today"? And then I realize. I'm next. Jasmine was today, and I'm next.

Chapter 2

When I wake up the next morning, there is a slip of paper on the floor. I glance around the room, and my gaze settles on the dark screen over the window between my cell and the cell next to mine. Not the one Jasmine was in. The other one. Unlike my old cell, the screens on the windows of this one do not come off, so I've never met this person in the adjacent cell. I only met Jasmine because we were on line for the showers together once. Anyway, I notice that there is a tiny crack on the screened window, and I realize that whoever this person is, they have sent me this paper.

I quickly get out of bed, the stone floor cool beneath my bare feet. Excitedly, I pick up the paper and unfold it.

> You are next. Then it is me. Don't ask how I know. I am going to escape. I know that you are one of the most powerful ones here. You have broken out of your cell before. If you are joining me, get out of your cell and meet me at the top of the steps right after you read this. When we escape, I know where we can go.
>
> —Talia, Cell 46

I don't know anyone named Talia, but if she's escaping, I'm definitely in. But then I begin to wonder. How the heck am I supposed to break down my door? I've tried so many times, I've lost count, and I've been unsuccessful every time since I've been in this new cell. How does Talia plan to break down her door? And how does she know the order of the people being taken? How is she planning to escape? Questions fill my mind.

No! *Focus!* I tell myself. I need to figure out how I'm going to get out of my cell. Shoving the note in my pocket, I look helplessly around the room, hoping something will spark an idea. My eyes settle on the space right next to the door. If I could get the guards to open the door, then maybe I could slip out invisibly... maybe I don't need to break the door down at all. This is only the beginning of an idea, but, for now, that has to be good enough. I take a deep breath, and form a fireball. I concentrate hard, and it grows. I throw it at the wall, knowing that it won't do anything but create a really strong burning smell. Good. That's what I want to happen. Next, I lift the bed using my mind, smashing it against the wall, making a loud crashing noise. As if on cue, footsteps thud outside my cell.

"Cell 47, prisoner, stand back! You are forbidden from practicing or using magic!" shouts a voice.

The guards are here, and everything is going according to my plan. I creep over to the door, pressing myself up against the wall next to it. Then, I concentrate as hard as I possibly can, until my left arm disappears. Then my right. Where my arms once were, all I see is the dark stone floor.

"Come on," I mutter.

My right leg vanishes from sight. When I escape, I'll find Artemis, and we'll be together again. But I can't do that if I can't turn invisible. My left leg vanishes. I hear the lock click.

"You have caused us so much trouble, Prisoner 47. We were planning to take you away later this afternoon, but now is fine too," says one of the guards, as more locks click.

"We'll take her like we took her sister," laughs another guard.

I can tell that they are trying to make me mad, just for their own pleasure. And that's their mistake. The door starts to open, and I start to get really angry. They won't take me! And I am going to get out of here and find Artemis! The door opens all the way, and finally, the rest of my body disappears. That burst of emotion was exactly what I needed. *Thanks guards*, I think sarcastically.

"Where is she?!" cries a guard, rushing into the cell.

I slip out of the door unnoticed. I can't believe that worked! And then I bump into a guard at the bottom of the steps.

"Hey! I think she's somewhere over here!" he shouts urgently.

"I don't see her!" another guard replies. "Do you think she is invisible?"

"Nonsense. Nobody her age with no training would be able to do that," says one of the guards, dismissing the idea as I rush to the top of the steps.

I don't see anyone. All that is there are huge, intimidating oak doors.

"Use the Locator!" orders a guard.

All of the guards reach into their weapon bags and pull out

small green orbs. They throw them up into the air, and the orbs all explode. The room fills with green light, and the air around me shimmers.

"There!" cries one of the guards, pointing at the shimmering air.

They still can't see me, but they know where I am because of the Locator. I wonder how it works. Can the Locator sense the magic? If I succeed in escaping, maybe I can learn more about it. Right now, though, I need to focus on the situation at hand. The guards charge towards me, and I try to unlock the doors at the top of the staircase. No luck. There is no key in sight, and tugging at the handles isn't doing any good. Then, I notice the air shimmering at the middle of the staircase. The guards stop, noticing it as well.

"Is it her?" one asks confusedly.

"No, the air is still shimmering up at the top," another replies.

It's strange that the air is shimmering at the middle of the staircase, because all that's there is a little bug. Unless...

The guards notice the bug.

"Smash it," I hear them say.

But before they can kill the bug, it transforms into a girl.

Chapter 3

Before the guards can even take out their zappers, the girl uses her mind to move all of their weapon bags toward her. Some of the guards reach for their bags as the straps lift off of their shoulders and into the air. The bags kind of remind me of the messenger bags worn by children selling papers back on the streets. I glance at the girl and can see that she is struggling, sweat beading on her forehead, but she keeps the bags moving until they are all next to her.

"Take them and get rid of them!" shouts the girl, brushing

her honey blonde hair out of her face.

Who is she talking to?

"Quickly!" she yells frustratedly as the guards call for reinforcements.

That's when I realize that she is talking to me. This must be Talia. But how can she see me? I look around me and notice that the air is still shimmering. Taking a deep breath, I use my mind to move the bags toward me.

"GET THE ONE AT THE TOP OF THE STEPS!" orders a guard.

Half of the guards charge toward me, weaponless. I try to think. Talia said to get rid of the bags, but how?

"INVISIBILITY!" screams Talia.

Huh? Oh! I guess if I can turn myself invisible, I can probably turn objects invisible too. I picture in my head the bags disappearing, and after a few seconds, the bags are gone. I use my telekinesis to scatter the invisible bags around the room. That should be good, at least until a guard bumps into their weapon bags. Then, we'll be in trouble.

"Don't try to fight them! Just get the door open!" Talia orders.

I nod, run to the door, and form a wall of bright orange fire around me. The guards jump back, coughing as they breathe in the smoky air. The comfort from the warmth and familiarity of my fire gives me strength. I can do this. I can get this door open. Although, I wonder why all of a sudden, I am so powerful. Before today, I could only get one arm to disappear, and then today I'm entirely invisible. And, I've never made a wall of fire before. How am I doing this? I can't focus on that right now, though. As I work to open the doors, the guards try to figure out how to get past my wall of fire. They will probably find a way soon, but for now, I have to focus on getting the door open. There is no lock, but when I try to simply pull it open, it doesn't budge. Then, I notice a small gray box by the door handle. There is a spot to put your finger on. So now, I need a guard's fingerprint. Great.

"Any luck?" Talia shouts.

"I need a fingerprint!" I respond, without turning away from the door. I clench my teeth, trying to stay calm.

"Don't lose concentration! Your wall of fire is fading!" Talia tells me.

I whirl around, just as the firewall vanishes. The guards race towards me. Or actually, towards the shimmering air. The guards are a step away from me when an idea forms. I look at the closest guard. Using my telekinesis, I move her next to the door and drop her there. I lift her finger towards the door, grunting with the effort. Sweat dripping down my forehead, I get her finger less than an inch away from the box when complete and total exhaustion hits me. My knees buckle, and I become visible again. Moving a person took way more energy than moving some bags. I don't have the strength to stay invisible, and they could see where I was anyway, thanks to the Locator.

"Talia! The fingerprint ... the guard by the door ... before she gets up ... " I yell, using the last of my strength to push the rest of the guards standing near me backward with my mind.

Talia somehow gets past the guards she was fighting and uses telekinesis to force the guard's finger onto the gray box. There is a click, and then the doors slowly creak open.

"Get up!" cries Talia urgently.

I try to stand, but my knees buckle again, and I fall back down. Clenching my teeth, I struggle to my feet, but my body is just too exhausted. I crumple to the ground, angry with myself. I shouldn't have moved the guard. I'm not strong enough for all of the magic I just did. Talia runs to my side and picks me up. Throwing me over her shoulder, she bolts out the door. I hear the heavy footsteps of the guards chasing us. We find ourselves in a long, cold hallway, different from the prisoner hallways. This hallway is cleaner, and more brightly lit. It makes me feel hopeful rather than doomed and dejected.

"Can you walk?" Talia asks, not slowing down.

"Yes," I lie.

She sets me down, and I stumble for a second and then fall.

"I thought you were supposed to be strong and powerful," Talia mutters in annoyance. "You have to get up. I can't keep carrying you, and the guards will catch up to us pretty soon. If we can just find—" She stops.

"Find who?" I say, forcing myself to stand, leaning against the wall for support.

Talia ignores my question. "You're too slow now. We'll never make it." She glances over her shoulder anxiously.

"I just need a few more minutes to get my energy back," I groan, collapsing to the floor again.

I am filled with embarrassment and shame knowing that I am going to be the reason that our escape fails. Because of me, not only will I be locked up again, but Talia will, too.

"Oh no," Talia says.

"What?" I ask her worriedly.

She points to the end of the hallway. Turning the corner is a guard, his eyes widening when he sees us.

"We have to run," decides Talia.

"Just leave me. I don't have the strength to run. I've never used that much magic at once before," I tell her.

Talia glances at me and then at the guard. "I wonder..."

She takes a tentative step toward the guard. I watch in confusion as the guard smiles. Upon seeing this, Talia's face lights up, and she runs toward the guard.

"Talia, what are you doing?!" I exclaim.

"Thank goodness it's you!" Talia cries, ignoring me.

She winces, glancing quickly over her shoulder to make sure nobody heard her. Then, she hugs the guard. What the heck?! Talia walks back over to me and the guard follows. He looks like he's only a few years older than me, with messy brown hair, dark skin, and twinkling brown eyes.

"Talia, what is going on? Why are you with a guard, and why isn't he attacking? Talia, you need to leave now, before the rest of the guards get here. One of us should get to escape and be free," I say to her.

"That's very noble of you," the guard standing next to Talia says, amusement in his voice.

"What are you waiting for, Talia? Go! Get out of here! I'll follow if I can," I beg her, ignoring the guard.

My head is spinning. Why isn't this guard attacking us, or locking us back up?

"Relax. This isn't a guard," Talia smiles.

"Then why is he wearing a guard uniform?" I demand, forcing my eyes to stay open. I feel like I'm going to pass out, and nothing is making sense through my cloud of exhaustion. But I need to at least try to stay focused.

"This is my boyfriend, JJ. He and I have been planning this escape for a while. He hasn't gotten caught and taken to the Marden yet, so he's been helping from the outside. He knows the way out because he's been stealing and studying maps of the place," explains Talia.

JJ interrupts, "We should really go. Like now."

"She has Fatiga," Talia explains to him.

"What's Fatiga?" I ask.

"It's the exhausted feeling you get when you use a lot of magic," JJ says quickly.

"Guys, the guards," I say, pointing at the mob of guards

coming down the hall. JJ throws me a water bottle, with a strange purple liquid inside of it.

"Drink this. It will give you your energy back for a few minutes. Catch up to us," JJ says, and he and Talia take off, sprinting away from the guards.

I drink as fast as I can and then I throw the bottle on the floor. After a moment, I feel my energy start to return. My head feels clearer and my limbs don't ache as much anymore. After a couple more seconds, I am able to successfully stand up. The guards are almost close enough to be able to zap me. I run at full speed in the direction JJ and Talia went, catching up to them a minute later. Talia looks surprised.

"How did you catch up so quickly?" she asks as we run, and I shrug in response.

"Guys, the Zoomer is at the end of this hallway," JJ tells us.

"Zoomer?" I reply.

"You know, the Transport vehicles Marden guards use," JJ says as if it is obvious.

We reach the end of the hallway, and I see the large, oval-shaped, green Zoomer sitting in an otherwise empty garage. The wheels are huge like they're meant for a bus instead of a small

Zoomer. It takes me a moment to even see where the door of the vehicle is because it completely blends in with the rest of the vehicle.

"Ok guys, get in," JJ orders.

But before I can move towards the door, there is a searing pain in my right shoulder. This is a very different feeling from the zapper. What did they shoot me with? I drop to the floor, terrified that if I close my eyes, I may never open them. But I am unable to stop my eyelids from drifting closed. The last thing I see is guards charging toward us, with their weapons out, and then the world goes black.

Chapter 4

I regain consciousness about 30 seconds later. Blurry figures move back and forth, and it takes a moment for the room to come into focus. When it does, the first thing I notice is Talia attempting to hold off the guards so that JJ can get the Zoomer started. I am surrounded by a shimmering force field, which I assume Talia or JJ put up. The second thing I notice is the throbbing pain in my right shoulder. Teeth clenched, I manage to get up off the floor. Along with the pain in my shoulder, my Fatiga is returning, but I think I still have enough energy to help Talia.

"Talia, break the forcefield!" I call out to her.

Talia ducks as one of the guards tries to paralyze her with a zapper.

"I can't right now. You have to break it yourself," she replies, and I can tell she is annoyed with me.

I guess I haven't been much help to her. In fact, I've slowed her down. I sigh and throw a fireball at the forcefield. The forcefield falters for a second, but doesn't break. I close my eyes, and a flicker of orange flame sparks to life in my palm. I pour all of my pent-up emotion, exhaustion, and energy into the fire. It grows and grows until it is almost engulfing my entire hand. I feel myself weakening, but I keep going. Opening my eyes, I throw the fireball at the forcefield. It shatters. The sound is deafening, even louder than the sound of the thunder that shook the Marden's walls on my first night there, and I put my hands over my ears. The guards stop fighting Talia, and cover their ears as well.

" TALIA, NOW!" I scream as loud as I can.

Talia and I sprint towards the Zoomer. It is only about 20 feet away from us, but it feels like a million miles.

"It's almost ready," JJ says nervously, as the guards start zapping again.

"JJ, hurry! That distraction did not buy us as much time as I had hoped it would," Talia says as we get into the vehicle.

She quickly creates a forcefield around the Zoomer.

"How much time do we have?" JJ asks, pressing different buttons inside the Zoomer.

I glance around the driver's area in amazement. I've never seen any place with so many gadgets and buttons. JJ is sitting in front of a metal board with about thirty different colored buttons, and he clearly has no idea which ones he's supposed to press.

"JJ, we probably have a minute. Their weapons are weakening the field, and it will definitely break soon. I'm also running out of energy," Talia tells him.

The Zoomer starts to beep loudly.

"Ok, it's ready," he says, and he starts to drive.

Talia and I stumble as the vehicle starts to move, and I hold onto the back of JJ's seat for support since there's nowhere in the driver's area for Talia and I to sit.

"Talia, press the yellow button. It will open the garage, and then we're out," JJ orders.

Talia hits the yellow button. Nothing.

"Try it again," JJ says, anxiously running his fingers through his hair.

I can tell he is panicking. Talia hits it again, but the garage door won't open.

"The forcefield is almost broken!" I cry anxiously.

Talia keeps hitting the button, but nothing happens.

"Can a guard lock the garage without being in a Zoomer?" I ask.

"I would assume so," Talia replies.

I look back at the guards. One of them is holding a small yellow remote. I point at her.

"Guys, look at what that guard is holding! It's the same color as the button. Maybe it's the guards' garage opener and closer. They probably carry one with them in case of escape," I say.

"That would make sense, but how are we going to get it?" JJ responds.

Suddenly, Talia collapses on the floor of the Zoomer.

"Uh oh," JJ says.

At that moment, the forcefield breaks. The deafening sound doesn't distract the guards this time, and they come charging forward.

"JJ, start driving," I order.

"But the garage door isn't open!" he protests.

"Just drive. Trust me!" I cry.

He starts driving. As he slowly inches towards the garage door, I use my mind to move the yellow remote out of the guard's hand and towards us. The guard reaches to grab it back, and I jerk it away.

"Duck!" JJ yells.

I duck, and a moment later, the window of the Zoomer shatters. I pop back up, and see that the remote is still floating towards me.

"JJ, should I make a forcefield?" I ask.

"Do you know how?" he replies.

"No," I mutter.

"Ok, well that decides it then," he says.

I turn my attention back to the guards. Their weapons are all aimed at me, and I must say, it is extremely difficult to focus on moving this remote with all these weapons shooting at me and trying to zap me.

"I can't go any further without crashing into the door," JJ calls out to me.

I don't respond and keep focusing on the remote. It is almost at the window of the Zoomer. And then, one of the zappers hits me. My body becomes paralyzed, and my concentration is broken completely. The remote drops, and a guard rushes forward to retrieve it. And as I fall to the ground, I know that all hope is lost. We're going to get captured. My vision gets blurry, and I feel like I'm going to pass out again. But right before I do, I see Talia get up off of the floor, and a couple seconds later, the yellow remote drops through the window. She pushes the button, and we're out.

ChaptEr 5

∾

When I wake up, Talia is standing over me. The bright lights on the ceiling of the Zoomer nearly blind me as I groggily push myself up onto my elbows.

"JJ, she's up!" Talia calls out.

"How long was I out?" I ask her.

"About an hour," she replies.

"I was passed out for an hour?!" I exclaim.

Talia nods.

"How did we get out? How'd you get the remote?" I say.

All I remember is Talia standing up, and the remote dropping through the window. But how did she get it?

"Can I talk to you guys?" asks JJ, before Talia can respond.

"Sure. Do you need help sitting up all the way?" she says to me.

I nod, and she helps me sit up. The room starts to spin, and I blink a couple times until it is back to normal.

Glancing at JJ, who is sitting in the driver area of the Zoomer, I notice that he is still dressed in a guard uniform.

"JJ, if you were wearing the guard uniform, how come they kept firing at us?" I ask.

"Well, I was trying to escape with you guys, so I think they realized I wasn't a guard," JJ replies.

"Oh," I say, feeling sort of stupid.

"We never asked you your name," Talia says to me, changing the subject.

"I'm Alavis."

"Alavis, how old are you?" she asks.

"14, if I'm remembering right," I tell her.

Talia and JJ look at each other.

"What?" I demand.

"I didn't really get a good look at you the day you broke out of your cell. You know, the day they took your sister. Well, I assume she was your sister. Anyway, I thought if you were strong and powerful enough to break out of your cell, you must be pretty old," Talia shrugs.

"How old are you two?" I ask her.

She says, "JJ and I are both 17."

"Oh," I say.

I'm starting to feel a bit like an outsider here. Talia and JJ already know each other, and every time I say something they glance at each other as if trying to make sense of me. I don't even know if I can really trust them. But I better figure that out soon.

"So Alavis—" Talia starts.

I cut her off.

"What was your plan? I understand that you were going to find JJ when you got out of our hallway, and he knew where a Zoomer was, and you were going to escape. But what exactly was your plan to get out of our hallway? Because it kind of felt like we were just winging it in there. You didn't even get to the top of the steps where we were supposed to meet," I question.

Talia sighs. "I have been working since the day I was brought to the Marden to master my shapeshifting. I finally mastered it and I was planning on turning into a tiny bug and sneaking out, unnoticed," begins Talia.

"Then why did you bring me along?" I snap.

She frowns. "I was getting there."

"Sorry," I say, trying not to let my temper get the best of me.

"I brought you along because if my plan didn't work, and we needed to fight, I thought it would be easier to have a second person to help me fight. I chose you because I thought you were super powerful. I mean, you had broken out of your cell. Sure, they caught you, but you still broke down the door and got to the staircase. Also, the other reason I wanted to escape with you was that, if you had trouble getting out of your cell unnoticed, you might cause a distraction and I could get out easier. Sorry," she says.

"It's fine," I shrug.

Inside though, I am angry. Talia basically wanted to sacrifice me to the guards, so that she could escape. Although, would I do the same thing if it meant saving Artemis? Sometimes I wonder how far I'm willing to go. I think I'd do most anything to protect my sister, but would I do it at the expense of others? This thought terrifies me. Will I have to make that choice at some point? Talia's voice jolts me out of my thoughts.

"No offense Alavis, but you kind of slowed me down," Talia tells me, a twinkle of annoyance in her sky blue eyes.

"Thanks," I mutter sarcastically, feeling my anger rise to the surface.

"Hey, I'm just being honest! I didn't expect you to get Fatiga that quickly, and that really slowed us down..." she says.

"Give her a break Talia. We're out now, and that's what matters," JJ interjects, giving Talia a pointed look in the rearview mirror.

I take a deep breath. "I'm sorry if I slowed you down Talia."

"It's ok. I guess JJ is right. We're out now, and that's what matters," she shrugs.

I glance out the window, watching the tall city buildings fly by. JJ says something but I can't seem to tear my eyes away from the window.

"Alavis!" JJ says, bringing my attention back to him and Talia. "We'll be arriving soon so I need to tell you both where we're going, and what is going to happen," he explains.

"Wait. First, I have a question," I interrupt.

"It can wait," JJ replies.

I was going to ask why sometimes my magic is really powerful, and sometimes I can barely get my arm to disappear, but I'll ask another time I guess. I cross my arms over my chest in annoyance.

"So, I was sleeping in an alleyway one night, and this kid came up to me. I punched him in the face, which was just because of instinct. It was dark, and I was worried a Marden guard had found me. Anyway, he didn't get annoyed. He said he understood, so I realized he was a magic kid too. He told me that he had been following me around the past couple days and that he saw me use some magic. So anyway, he said that he saw a letter I was writing to Talia. He told me that if we wanted to escape this planet, he knew a way we could. The kid said he would tell me if we let him escape with us," says JJ.

"Wait a second. Leave this planet?!" I exclaim.

"Oh yeah. Talia and I want to leave the planet," JJ tells me.

"And go where?" I cry.

"Masthinya," Talia says.

"What the heck is Masthinya?" I ask.

JJ laughs. "Have you never seen an image of our solar system?"

"No, I have not. I've been in the Marden since I was nine, and before that, I mostly lived on the streets. How have either of you seen an image of our solar system?" I scowl.

"Calm down Alavis. I'll explain," says Talia.

She takes a deep breath and begins.

"I've only been in the Marden for two years. Before that, JJ and I both lived on the streets. However, there was a woman who trained and taught us in secret. There are so few magic people that aren't in the Marden, so JJ and I were so lucky to find someone to teach us. She trained us to use our magic, and taught us about our planet and our solar system," she explains.

Talia grabs a pad of paper and a pen from the glove compartment of the Zoomer. She draws six medium-sized circles surrounding a larger circle.

"In the center is Brightstar. It is what gives all the planets light and heat," Talia tells me.

She writes a B inside the circle in the center. Then, she labels the rest of the planets.

"These are the planets in our solar system. Caldoria: our planet, Masthinya: the planet where magic people are welcomed, Camden: the animal planet, Zathen and Denima: the two other planets like ours, that have both magic and non-magic people, and Elvaqua; the worst planet," she teaches me.

"Why is Elvaqua the worst planet?" I ask.

Talia shrugs. "I don't know. The woman who taught us just said it was the worst planet."

"Why are Zathen, Denima, and Caldoria all in that same little area, and everything else is far away?" I inquire.

Talia glances at the paper. "Those three planets are really close to each other. Masthinya is a little farther, and Elvaqua is close to Masthinya and Camden."

"Oh, got i—"

JJ interrupts me, the annoyance clear in his voice. "Hey, guys? You never let me finish telling you where we are going."

"You said we're going to Masthinya," I respond.

JJ looks about ready to kill me. "Wouldn't you like to know how we are getting there?" JJ scowls.

"Yes, sorry," I say.

"Carter and I—"

"Who is Carter?" I ask.

"Carter is the kid who said he would help Talia and I escape," JJ explains.

"Oh ok."

"So, Carter found the Marden's field, where a bunch of their spaceships are. It's got a ton of security around it, but Carter is a literal genius, and he figured out how to hack the system. We have to meet him at the field, and then he'll hack in, get the security system off, take the ship and we'll go to Masthinya," JJ says.

"Does Carter know that we have Alavis with us too?" Talia asks.

"Yeah. I said you might be escaping with another person," JJ replies.

"Okay. How far is the field?" Talia says.

"Not far. We're really close now. I think," says JJ, looking at the electronic map to his right.

I can't believe we're really going to get off this planet and are going to live on a planet where we're welcomed. Out of habit, I start to fidget with my bracelet. Except instead of my fingers touching the familiar string, all I feel is my bare wrist. My bracelet is gone. Tears start to form in my eyes as I realize that I must have lost it during the escape. I can't believe I lost Artemis' bracelet!

Oh my goodness. Artemis. My heart skips a beat, and my face turns pale.

"Alavis, are you ok?" Talia asks, worriedly.

"Artemis. I need to find her!"

Chapter 6

I jump out of my seat and race past JJ, towards the door of the Zoomer. I pull at it, trying to get it open but it doesn't budge.

"JJ, unlock the door," I order.

"You are not seriously planning to jump out of a moving vehicle, are you?" he replies.

"I am. I need to find my sister," I say.

Talia comes over to me, her manner far gentler than I've seen since I met her.

"Alavis, how are you going to find her?"

"I don't know! But I have to try!" I cry, continuing to pull at the door.

"It won't open unless I unlock it," JJ tells me.

I stomp over to him. "Unlock the door."

"No."

"Don't you understand that I need to search for my sister?!" I exclaim frustratedly.

"Alavis, I understand that you love your sister and want to find her. But you wandering the streets looking for her is just going to land you back in the Marden," he sighs.

"Why do you care what I do? I just met you! Now, unlock the door," I scowl.

JJ doesn't reply, and I glare at him, forming a fireball in my palm.

"Open it, or I'll make you," I warn, stepping closer so that I am right next to him.

Fear flickers in JJ's eyes for just a moment, and then he raises his eyebrows.

"Alavis, you're going to use up your energy," he says.

"She's my sister. I have to at least try to find her. If she's somewhere on this planet, and we leave, I may never see her again!"

I shout, trying to make him understand.

"Look, I—" JJ starts to say.

But before he can finish, I realize that fire is not my only power that could be helpful right now. Using my telekinesis, I force his finger to flip the unlock switch. I race to the door, and hop out of the Zoomer, landing on the hard concrete of the street. Suddenly, looking at the vastness of the city around me, I am incredibly overwhelmed. How will I ever find where Artemis is? I glance back at Talia and JJ, who are debating in hushed voices whether to come with me or not. Who cares? They can do whatever the heck they want, but I'm going to find out where Artemis is. No matter how difficult that might be. Although, I don't really have a plan, so I'll just have to wing it. Before starting down the street, I turn myself invisible, which takes a few minutes, and a whole lot of energy. If I end up having to fight, which is likely, I won't have much energy left. I sigh. I'll cross that bridge when I get to it.

Down the street, I spot a clothing store, and I know that's where I'm heading first. I don't think I'll have the energy to stay invisible for long, and obviously, once I'm visible, I can't be in my prisoner uniform, or people will know I'm a Marden escapee. Then, the guards will be called, and I'll be locked up again. After slipping into the store unnoticed, I scan the shelves, my eyes widening at all the different styles of clothing. It's been so long since I've worn anything but gray jumpsuits. A woman walks into the store, plucking a dark green blouse and a long green skirt off the rack. She heads into a dressing room, a little girl trailing behind her. I keep scanning the shelves, my eyes settling on a bright purple dress. Before I can take it off the shelf, I shake my head. I don't want to stand out. Sighing, I grab a pale blue tank top and black jeans. Very simple, very ordinary. I also grab a pair of sneakers. There is a garbage bin right outside the store, so after changing I drop my prisoner uniform in.

"Alavis!" a voice whispers.

I turn in a circle, but all I see are empty sidewalks. This doesn't seem to be a very busy street. The heat from Brightstar beats down on my face, and I keep searching for the person who called my name.

"It's me. Talia. This is extremely stupid of you by the way. But I feel like I can't just let you do this alone. Just know that if we get captured, I will kill you. Anyway, JJ is waiting at the Zoomer, ready to take off when we get back," explains the voice.

I still don't see anyone.

"Where are you?" I ask quietly.

"Invisible, same as you. I'm going to run in and change my outfit. I assume that's why you went into the clothing store. Anyway, where are we going when I'm done changing?" Talia replies.

"I ... I don't know. Who would know where the people taken from the Marden were brought?" I say.

"Guards would know," Talia sighs.

I groan. "How are we going to ask a guard without getting captured?"

There is no response. I guess she went into the store.

"Ok, I'm back," Talia says a couple minutes later.

"All right. So how are we going to ask a guard?" I sigh.

"I guess we just find one who is patrolling the streets. They won't know we're magic," Talia suggests.

"I don't have a better idea," I shrug, trying to hide my growing panic.

I'm going to have to go up to a Marden guard. I find myself having trouble breathing. I need to remember that despite my fears, I have to do this. This is for Artemis.

"For Artemis," I murmur under my breath.

My panic subsides a little.

"Okay. Let's go find a guard," Talia says, grabbing my hand.

She leads me down the street, toward an area crowded with people rushing by, bags on their arms. There are Zoomers driving by, people riding bicycles, and couples walking hand in hand. But that is only the surface of the city. If I look a little more closely, I see young children with dirt-covered faces hiding in every nook and cranny, eyes searching the streets for guards. Artemis and I used to be those children.

I truly never thought I would be trying to find a guard. I mean, my childhood was spent running from the Marden guards, and then being locked up by them. My heart aches as I remember Darren, a boy from the streets who was like a brother to me. He was taken to the Marden before Artemis and me. I wonder if he's still there.

All of a sudden, a shrill cry catches my attention. Turning down the side street where the noise came from, I see two guards hauling a little boy down the street. Talia nudges me, and we both turn visible.

"We are non-magic civilians, who despise people that have magic," Talia murmurs to me, and I nod.

"Excuse me, sir," Talia says as we come up behind the guards.

They stop and turn around. My heart pounds in my chest and

the walls of the shadowy street feel like they are closing in on me.

"Who are you girls?" one of them says in a gruff voice.

"Nobody important. Just some non-magic city folk," shrugs Talia, trying to seem nonchalant.

"Smooth," I mutter under my breath.

Talia elbows me in the stomach.

"Ow!"

"And what do you 'unimportant city folk' want? We're in the middle of something," snaps the other guard.

As if on cue, the little boy whimpers. Poor kid.

"We heard a rumor that they're taking people from the Marden and sending them somewhere else. My friend and I were curious about where they were being taken," I say with an innocent smile.

"Our job is not to answer the inquiries of irrelevant children," says the first guard.

"We want to know, if you please. It will only take a second to answer," I reply.

"Why do you care?" grumbles the second guard.

The first guard exchanges a look with the second guard.

"Use the gem."

Chapter 7

Guard number one pulls out a sparkling purple gem. Seeing it gives me a flashback to the day Artemis and I were captured.

We had been asking Mel, the hot dog guy, for free hotdogs. He had finally agreed, and as he was making them, the guards appeared out of nowhere. They asked where our parents were. I remember lying and saying that they were waiting for us back at the house. They obviously didn't buy it. Why would a parent send their five and nine year old out onto the streets by themselves? Then one guard had pulled out a purple gem, and the other guard had grabbed my arm and touched the gem to it. The gem turned a deep red color. It then turned back to purple, and the guard did the same to Artemis. It turned red again.

"Magics," he had muttered. They took us away.

I murmur, "Talia, it's the—"

"I know."

Guard one grabs my arm, and attempts to touch the gem to it. Before she can, I knee her in the stomach. She stumbles backwards, slamming into guard number two. Using my telekinesis, I push them both to the ground, and then, instinctively, a fireball forms in my hand. I guess it doesn't really matter anymore if the gem touches my arm. I think they know we're magic by now. The guards get up, knocking over a pair of garbage cans and a bicycle in the process, and point their zappers at us.

"We're taking you two to the Marden," guard one says.

"Let's just throw them on the spaceship, and take them to where the others were taken. It's so much easier that way," guard two suggests to the first guard.

Talia's eyes widen, and she whispers, "Alavis, they're not on this planet."

The second guard puts his hands over his mouth, realizing

what he's given away.

"What planet?!" I demand, as Talia forms a forcefield around us.

Guard one gives us an evil smile.

"None of your business. Allen, let's just kill them," guard one says.

"We can't, Liz. All Marden guards have the order: All magics shall be taken to the Marden, no exceptions. No killing," guard two, Allen, replies.

"The boss won't know," guard one, Liz, shrugs.

She switches weapons. This weapon is a bit larger, but otherwise looks the same as the cylinder-shaped, gray zapper. Except, I have a feeling this one won't just paralyze us.

"Alavis, I can't hold it any longer," Talia tells me as the forcefield disappears. Liz's finger starts to push down on the trigger, and I rip the weapon out of her hands using my telekinesis.

"What planet were they taken to?!" I shout.

Allen raises his weapon.

"Don't move," he warns.

"WHERE?!" I scream, attempting to throw his weapon down the street.

But after seeing this happen to Liz, he is prepared. He holds on tight to the weapon.

"Call reinforcements," Allen orders.

Liz pulls a small rectangular piece of metal out of her pocket. She presses a few buttons, and then a holographic image pops up. A woman with short, neatly cut, dark green hair, is sitting at a desk.

"Yes?"

"We need reinforcements," Liz explains, pointing the image at us.

"Reinforcements are on their way. Don't let them go. These are the escapees," the woman replies.

I hurl a fireball at the metal rectangle in Liz's hand. She drops it quickly to avoid getting burnt.

"Alavis, we have to get out of here," Talia says.

"Not until I find out where she was taken!" I respond, my blood boiling.

"They won't tell you! You're no good to your sister if you're dead or locked up!" Talia yells.

"I need to know where she is!" I shout, on the verge of tears.

"We need to g—" she pauses. "Alavis, move!"

I jump out of the way as Allen's bullet grazes my arm. The

pain is bad. Really bad. The kind of pain that feels as if a trillion knives are stabbing into your arm. But I can't leave until I know where Artemis is, so I clench my teeth and try to ignore the pain.

"What planet?!" I scream, attempting to create a wall of fire around me. It holds for about two seconds, and then the fire slowly disappears. My head is spinning, and my vision starts to get blurry. I glance at my arm, and the sight of my blood makes me nauseous. I feel like I'm going to throw up, or pass out. I end up doing the latter. I stumble, and collapse on the floor, my head hitting the hard ground.

"Alavis? We have to go! Alavis! Alavis ... Alavis." Talia's voice gets fainter and fainter, until I can't see or hear her, or anyone.

Chapter 8

My eyes fly open, and I quickly look around me. Talia is carrying me, running as fast as she can. In the distance, the green zoomer is parked in an alleyway, waiting for us. Behind us, the guards are on our tail. I realize that there is a forcefield moving with Talia and me as we run.

"Come on. Almost there," she mutters.

"I can run, Talia. Set me down," I tell her.

My arm is killing me, and I'm exhausted, but I don't want to make Talia carry me.

"Okay. When I put you down, do not stop. You should be running the second your feet hit the ground, ok?" Talia says.

I nod, and she puts me down. Immediately, I start running, each step feeling like I am running uphill with a 300-pound weight on my back.

"We're so close," Talia pants.

I can see JJ's face through the window of the Zoomer. Almost there.

"Don't let them get away," the guard Allen cries out.

I sneak a peek over my shoulder and see that the two guards are getting dangerously close to us.

"Alavis!" Talia cries out.

I glance at her and see she is frozen in place a few feet behind me. The paralyzing weapon. Shoot. Her forcefield shatters.

Panicking, I look around me. It is a maze of tall buildings and crowded streets, and I fear that if I run down different streets trying to lose the guards, I'll never find my way back to the Zoomer.

So, I have to get Talia, and myself, to that Zoomer. Now.

"JJ!" I yell as I lift Talia's body into the air with my mind.

I manage to get her a foot off the ground, but I don't think I can move her. I have to get her into the Zoomer before the guards catch up.

"TALIA!" JJ comes running towards us.

He lifts her up and carries her to the Zoomer. I use my telekinesis, and the last of my strength, to get the weapons out of Liz and Allen's hands.

"Get in, Alavis. Quickly," JJ shouts urgently.

I dash inside, locking the doors behind me, while JJ starts driving.

"Can you go faster?" I beg.

"If I could, I would."

I flop down in one of the seats in the back of the Zoomer, beyond tired. Talia's paralyzation has mostly worn off now because thankfully the weapons only paralyze for a short period of time. She comes over to inspect my injury, shaking out her legs and arms to get rid of the after-effects of the paralysis.

"JJ, is there a medical kit?" she asks.

"There should be one in the little box by Alavis' seat."

Talia opens up a small white box from below my seat and pulls out some medical tools. She starts to clean up the bullet wound on my arm.

"Ow, that hurts!" I cry.

"What do you want me to do, let it get infected?" Talia mutters.

"No, no. Keep going. Thanks, Talia," I say, wincing.

"No problem," she replies.

My eyelids grow heavy, and I fall asleep, dreaming of reuniting with Artemis.

* * *

"So, we'll be at the field pretty soon. And I wouldn't be surprised if those Marden guards followed us, so be ready to fight," JJ says when I wake up.

"Wait, what field? Huh?" I reply groggily.

JJ sighs. "The field. With the spaceships? We're meeting Carter there."

"Carter? Who— Oh, right. Right," I say, blinking a couple times to try to make myself more alert and awake.

"JJ, do you have any more Fatiga Juice?" Talia asks him, yawning.

"A little. It's in the glove compartment," he responds.

Talia digs around in the glove compartment, and after a couple seconds, she pulls out a plastic bottle. Inside is the purple liquid that JJ gave me earlier. There's only a tiny bit in it.

"We'll each take a small sip," Talia says.

"I had to use up most of the money I had, which was not a lot, to get this. I knew we would need it, but it's really hard to come by," JJ tells us, as Talia takes a sip.

"Why is it so hard to come by?" I ask.

"You've got to know how to make it. So few people know how, and even if you did, the ingredients are all really rare stuff," he explains.

"So it's like … a potion?" I inquire.

He answers, "Yeah sort of."

Talia hands the bottle to me. "Only a tiny bit," she repeats.

I nod, take a small sip, and give it to JJ.

"Wait. Doesn't it only last a few minutes?" I say worriedly.

"Good thing we're here," JJ replies.

He parks the Zoomer, and we get out. Anxiously glancing around for guards, JJ walks up to the tall electric fence surrounding the big grassy field. On the field, there are 10 huge spaceships sitting on launchpads. I can't believe I'm going to get to fly in one of those.

"Carter?" JJ whispers.

Looking back at us, JJ points at a tall metal tower, "Carter should be coming from there. That's where the switch for the electric fence is. At least, I think so, based on the map that Carter and I studied."

While JJ continues to look for Carter, Talia closes her eyes. She leans her head back, her arms outstretched.

"What are you doing?" I laugh.

"I'm trying to turn into a bird but it's not working," she says nervously.

"Didn't you say it took years for you to master shapeshifting?" I ask.

She nods.

"Does it take a lot of strength and energy?" I continue.

She nods again, waiting for me to get to the point.

"Well, we just fought off a bunch of guards, and used a ton of magic, so maybe you don't have the strength right now," I say. "And besides, why are you wasting all your energy on trying to turn into a bird?"

Talia just sighs. "Come on," she mutters to herself, as she continues to try to shapeshift.

It's like she didn't even hear me.

"Guys! I found Carter!" JJ whisper-shouts.

He returns to where we are standing with a boy that looks to be around my age. He has curly chestnut brown hair, chestnut brown eyes, and olive skin.

"I'll make introductions quickly because we really don't have time," JJ says. He points at Talia. "Carter, this is Talia." He points to me next. "And this is Alavis."

"Nice to meet you guys," he replies, smiling at us quickly.

I suddenly feel myself wishing I had brushed my hair this morning. I mean, I didn't really have time to, but still. Talia nudges me.

"Alavis, you're staring," she whispers.

My cheeks turn red, and I look away.

"So, Carter, have you hacked the security system yet?" JJ asks.

Carter nods.

"Yup. That control tower was a lot more intense than I was expecting, but I figured it out. No alarms should go off. No one should get electrocuted. We're all set." He adds, "Hopefully."

"I love not getting electrocuted," JJ grins.

"Okay. I guess we just walk up to the ship," Talia says.

Nobody moves. We stand there for a minute, and then Talia takes a step forward, pushing open the gate. I'm about to follow, when a small gray kitten bursts onto the field, running out of a forest to the left of us. She streaks past, meowing loudly in fear. The kitten runs onto the ship, and we all turn in the direction the cat came from. Guards.

ChaptER 9

❧

"Do we make a run for it?" asks Carter, glancing nervously at the guards, who are a couple hundred feet away.

Looking around at each of us, then at the field of spaceships, Carter adds, "Or fight?" His voice quivers a little bit.

"Run," JJ says, at the same time that Talia says, "Fight."

"Uh ... how about both?" I say, as the guards aim their weapons at us.

Talia forms a forcefield, but we all know it won't protect us for long. And I know that the Fatiga Juice will wear off pretty quickly too.

"Who here knows how to get the ship started? Please tell me someone knows how," Talia asks.

"Not me. I've been in the Marden since I was nine. They don't teach spaceship courses there," I say.

JJ and Talia both glare at me.

"This is not the time for jokes," Talia says.

"Sorry."

"I can start it," Carter says.

"You can?" Talia asks, her eyebrows raised skeptically.

"I'm the one who hacked their security system. I promise I can start the ship— well, I think I can."

Beneath his brave mask, I can see the fear in Carter's eyes.

"Okay. Carter, get the ship started then. JJ and I will fight them off here. In case some get past us, Alavis, stand guard by the ship. Don't let anyone near the ship, or inside of it. Yell to us when it's ready to go," Talia orders.

"Okay, I will," I promise.

Talia breaks the forcefield, and Carter sprints to the ship. He goes inside, and I stand by the entrance. I don't know how to make a forcefield, or if I even have that ability for that matter, so I need to figure something else out.

A guard runs towards me, aiming his zapper at my chest. But before he can reach me, I get an idea. I throw a fireball at him to slow him down and focus on creating a wall of fire around the ship. The flames dance along the edges of the sleek ship, singing the hairs off the arms of those unfortunate few who are nearby. When the orange flames are almost all the way around the ship, I feel a sort of tingle in my left leg, and then it goes numb. Well, at least the zapper only paralyzed my leg and not my whole body. I finish the firewall, and hop back towards the entrance. A guard charges into the wall of fire, and I wince as I smell the burning flesh. Although they are trying to capture us, I still feel horrible for hurting them. They are still people after all ...

A moment later, the guard reaches me, badly burnt. He points his zapper at me. I'm already feeling weak from creating the whole firewall, but I try to lift him off the ground using telekinesis. I do not succeed and end up dropping him on the ground. He gets back up, his weapon still pointed at me. I form a fireball, using the little bit of strength I still have.

"Put the fire away, and I will not use this weapon on you," he says.

Yeah, right, I think to myself. Desperately, I try to think of a way to distract him, so Carter can keep working on getting the ship started. If I throw the fireball at the guard, he'll likely paralyze me, or shoot me, or something. Suddenly, the gray kitten that burst onto the field earlier comes out of the ship. I quickly use telekinesis, and close the door behind it. I don't want to have the poor kitten hurt by the guard, but I can't leave the door open, or the guard will get in. The guard pulls out a second zapper and points it at the cat.

"Is it one of you?" he demands.

"I don't know," I reply truthfully.

I feel lightheaded, like I'm about to faint. The Fatiga Juice basically already wore off, but I keep the fireball in the palm of my hand. It's tiny and would probably only cause a small burn, but I don't have the strength to make it stronger.

"Just make your fire vanish, and I will put the weapon away," the guard repeats, and I don't reply.

"Fine," he says.

I realize that he is about to pull the trigger and paralyze me (or shoot me; I don't really know which zappers do what), but I throw the fireball before he can. It hits his hand, causing him to drop the zapper. He backs up, away from me.

"READY!" Carter screams.

I hear it, but I don't know if Talia and JJ do.

"READY!!!" I yell to them.

"OKAY! GET RID OF THE WALL OF FIRE!" JJ yells back.

I close my eyes, and imagine the firewall vanishing. I open my eyes, and see that it is gone. The guard bolts off into the woods, clutching his burnt hand, and JJ and Talia turn themselves invisible. A couple seconds later, I feel a tap on the shoulder.

"Get on." It's Talia.

We all rush onto the oval-shaped, sleek gray and white ship, and the kitten follows us on.

"All right. We're about to take off," Carter calls out.

"Guys! There's a guard trying to get on the ship!" JJ cries.

I look through the ship's window, and see a guard tugging at the door.

"Carter, quickly!" Talia says.

"Is it locked?" I ask.

"Shoot. I forgot to lock it," JJ says.

I rush over to the door, but I'm too late. Before I can lock it, the guard opens the door. He zaps me, and I fall to the cold, metal floor, paralyzed. I wonder why he paralyzed me and didn't just kill me. I guess they don't want to kill me. They just want to take me back to the Marden. But now isn't the time to ponder that because the guard is now aiming his zapper at Talia and JJ. However, before he can shoot, the weapon freezes. Like literally freezes. The door suddenly pushes open, and the guard is shoved out, as if by an invisible hand. The door closes, and locks. We start to take off, and my stomach drops. Talia walks forward.

"Who's there?" she demands.

"Hey! Who's there?" she repeats.

A hand appears by the door, and then another. Finally, after a minute, the person becomes fully visible. It's a little girl, and she's holding a dagger.

Chapter 10

"Please don't kill me," she says in a small voice, her lower lip quivering.

"Who are you?" Talia asks, her voice hard.

"Zoë Daelen," the little girl tells us.

"Do we know if we can trust her?" I whisper to Talia.

"I can hear you, you know. I just want to escape," says Zoë, as a tear rolls down her cheek.

JJ walks over to her and says, "I've seen you on the streets."

"Meaning we should just trust her?" Talia snaps.

"What are you going to do? Throw her off the ship? We're in the air, Talia!" JJ argues.

As they argue, I walk over to the door, where Zoë is standing. There are a bunch of shiny metal seats right past where Talia and JJ are, but at the moment we are all crowded by the spaceship door, trying to figure out what to do about Zoë.

I kneel down next to the little girl. "I'm Alavis. Were you the kitten we saw?" I ask her in a kind voice.

She nods, anxiously tugging at a strand of her curly red hair.

"That's pretty cool that you can shapeshift," I smile, trying to get her to relax a little.

"My mommy could shapeshift. So could my daddy," Zoë tells me, her voice trembling.

I reply, keeping my expression happy and friendly. "That's so cool. I wish I could shapeshift."

Zoë swallows hard, tears forthcoming, just waiting for the dam to break. After a couple seconds, it does break, and a steady stream of tears are falling down her cheeks.

"What's wrong?" I say, trying to keep my voice gentle and kind.

"The guards ... they came and were going to take me and my

parents to the Marden ... but my mommy and daddy fought off the guards so I could escape ... I just miss them ... " Zoë sobs.

My eyes sting with tears. As I look at the crying girl in front of me, I think that this could be Artemis somewhere. Sobbing, with nobody to comfort her.

I give Zoë a hug. "Have you been living alone?"

"I've been living on the streets, by myself, for a couple months now. I saw these two boys plotting an escape." She pauses and points at JJ. "He was one of them. I decided to go to the field they talked about, so I could get off of this awful planet, too," she sniffles.

I pick her up and start to carry her over to where Carter is flying the ship. Talia and JJ's arguing has gotten louder, and the poor girl shouldn't have to hear it.

"Do you want to go meet the boy who's flying the ship?" I say.

"Okay. But I know you're just taking me there so the boy and girl can argue about me, and decide if they're going to kill me," Zoë responds.

"You're a smart one, Zoë," I tell her. "Talia and JJ just want to be safe. I won't let them kill you, okay?"

"Okay," she says.

Heading through the doorway into the cockpit of the ship, I

sit down in the seat next to Carter and pull Zoë onto my lap.

"Hi Alavis," he says, not looking up from the controls.

"Hi. Carter, this is Zoë. Zoë, this is Carter," I introduce them.

Carter glances up at Zoë. "How old are you?"

"I'm six," she says, watching as Carter grips the tiller, turning it left and right to steer the ship.

He pushes a couple buttons and then pulls a bright blue lever. To be honest, I have no clue how he knows what buttons and levers to use, since there are hundreds of buttons, and about twenty different levers, all throughout the cockpit.

Zoë clears her throat. "Um, are you going to be sitting here, pressing buttons, and steering the whole time? Do you even know where you're going?"

"I know what I'm doing," Carter says, a hint of annoyance in his voice.

Zoë shakes her head. "Move over."

When Carter doesn't move, Zoë unbuckles the seatbelt and pushes him out of the seat using telekinesis. She then waves her hand in the air and a misty purple figure forms.

"Fly this ship. Take us to ... " she starts.

"Masthinya," Carter tells her.

"Take us to Masthinya," Zoë orders.

The figure sits down and starts to steer the ship. How is a six-year-old that good at magic? Did she have training? I doubt it ...

"That was really cool, Zoë. Thanks," Carter smiles.

"No problem. Now you don't have to work the ship the whole time. It will probably be a long trip," she says, the excitement of showing us her powers clear on her face.

Carter, Zoë, and I head out of the cockpit and back over to Talia and JJ, who are still standing by the spaceship's door.

"You guys done arguing?" I ask.

"We're not arg— yeah we're done," Talia says.

"Fantastic. Zoë, this is Talia and JJ. Talia and JJ, this is Zoë. You will not lock her up somewhere on the ship, and you will not harm her in any way. She is our friend," I say.

Talia and JJ both glare at me.

"It's our decision, Alavis," says JJ.

"Why?" I demand.

"Because ... we're older."

I shrug. "So?"

"Alavis, why are you so sure that we can trust her? You don't know her!" Talia exclaims.

"Hey! People, I'm standing right here. Nice to meet you. Beautiful day today, no?" Zoë says sarcastically.

"See, Alavis? The innocent, sweet little girl was obviously an act. She could be a spy for the guards!" Talia says.

"I pushed a guard out the door," Zoë reminds us.

I sigh in exasperation. "Talia, you need to relax. Zoë's not going to hurt us."

"Fine. I'm sorry, Zoë. I'm just very scared that everything is a trap. I don't want to end up back in the Marden, or worse," says Talia, a touch of bitterness still in her voice.

"I understand. But I'm really not a spy for the guards. I just want to escape to somewhere safe," Zoë replies.

Talia suddenly notices Carter standing next to Zoë.

"Carter, if you're here, who's flying the ship?!" Talia cries.

"Zoë's magic figure," I say.

"Ah, well that clears it right up," JJ says, and I roll my eyes.

I shrug. "Go look."

JJ and Talia go to the cockpit, and while they're there, I think about where Artemis could be. There are too many planets to choose from. Where do I start?

"Nice work, Zoë," JJ grins, coming through the doorway, out

of the cockpit.

"You've got skills," Talia agrees, looking at the little girl with admiration.

A smile spreads across Zoë's face. "Thanks!"

"Guys, I need to talk to you about something ... I don't think we should go to Masthinya," I say.

JJ's eyebrows furrow in confusion. "What do you mean?"

"Well, why would my sister have been taken to the planet where magic people are welcomed? That's the least likely option. It's got to be one of the other planets," I explain.

JJ and Talia exchange a look.

"What?" I demand.

"We know you want to find your sister, Alavis ... and we want to help you. But just listen to reason for a second. We have a better chance of finding her if we go to Masthinya first. We can rest up for a couple nights, get some supplies, maybe get a group together to help us find her," Talia says.

"What if she's dead by then?" I ask, my voice shaking. Tears start to roll down my cheeks.

"You want to go charging onto a planet you've never been to, with no weapons, and only three teenagers, and a six-year-old, with you for help?" Talia asks. "Besides, didn't the guards say they weren't allowed to kill people with magic? That they had to take them to the Marden alive? So your sister should still be alive if we wait a few days more."

I know she's right. I remember the guards saying that ... But that was on Caldoria. Things could be different wherever Artemis is. But still, Talia and JJ are right that I'll have a better chance of helping Artemis if we stop at Masthinya first.

"A few days. We can stay there a few days, long enough to get together some people to help us, gather some supplies, and then we're leaving. Or, I am. You guys don't have to come with me. I'm not going to make you put yourself in danger if you don't need to," I say.

"We're coming with you," Carter tells me.

"You really don't need to. I'll be fine," I insist.

I'd like to have them with me, but I don't want to put them in danger. We just escaped the Marden. They should get to relax.

JJ shrugs. "We're coming, whether you like it or not."

"All right. Thanks," I reply gratefully.

Zoë clears her throat.

"Yes?" Talia asks.

"Um, that was sweet and all, but shouldn't we sit down, and

put on seat belts?" Zoë suggests.

As if on cue, the ship lurches forward, and we all fall to the ground.

Chapter 11

O nce we've all sat down in the cold metal chairs that surround the dull gray table and put on our seat belts, the Fatiga hits me. I don't know why it took so long, but now I am exhausted, and I have to fight to keep my eyes open. I hear JJ suggest that we get to know each other.

"I'll start," he says. "I'm JJ, which you guys obviously already know. I'm 17 years old, and I've been living on the streets my whole life. They don't sell houses to us magic people, as I'm sure you all know. I met Talia when I was 10, and we found a lady to train us to use our magic. The lady eventually got caught and was taken to the Marden. They took both Talia and her, but I got away. That was when Talia and I were 15. Talia and I have been planning her escape ever since."

"What about your parents?" I ask.

"They were taken to the Marden when I was a baby," he says sadly, his dark eyes brimming with tears.

"Oh. I'm sorry," I reply.

"We've all got tough lives, Alavis. Where are your parents?" he asks quietly.

"Dead. At least, I think they are. One day, they handed me my little sister, who was an infant at the time, and said 'Take good care of her. We'll miss you both so much.' They left. I don't know where they went, but they never came back." I say, fighting back tears.

I don't share the rest of what my parents said to me that day with the group. It hurts too much. The memory of my mother telling me, "I promise we will be back, Alavis," is too painful.

Because they never did come back.

"Your father and I are trying to make a better life for you. We're trying to give you a better life than you'll get here," I remember her saying.

I squeeze my eyes shut tight, longing for my family. Despite being surrounded by people right now, I feel so alone. But I also feel angry. Why didn't my parents take Artemis and me with them? Why did they leave us all alone, with nobody but each other, to fend for ourselves? What kind of parents do that? Actually, I vaguely remember my parents leaving us with a woman, but she got taken to the Marden a few days after my parents left. So though I suppose they did leave us in the care of someone else, and they didn't know she would get taken away right after they left, why did they have to leave at all?

"They could still be alive somewhere," Carter offers.

I sigh, wiping away the tears trailing down my cheeks. "Maybe. I don't know. I doubt it."

Talia unbuckles her seatbelt and comes over to me, putting her arm around my shoulder. We stay that way in silence for a few minutes.

"At least there's still a chance of you finding your sister. My whole family is dead," Carter mumbles, his eyes glued to the floor.

"What happened to them?" Talia asks, moving back to her seat.

"My parents died when my sister and I were both very young,

so my sister raised me. Then, she died on the streets when I was 10. She was 16. We were starving, it was cold, and she got sick. Of course, magic people that get sick are doomed, but I refused to accept that. I searched and searched, and finally, I found a doctor who was willing to secretly help her. But, it was too late," Carter tells us, his eyes red.

"What was your sister's name?" I say.

"Saige. I miss her so much," he replies, his voice breaking.

"I'm so sorry, Carter," I say.

He doesn't say anything, silence filling the room.

"I'm going to go get some rest," Talia announces suddenly, breaking the silence.

"Me too," yawns Zoë.

Talia gets out of her seat, heading down the hallway to the right. She pushes open a heavy metal door, peering into the first room. I catch a glimpse of a sink and a toilet. Bathroom. Talia opens the next door, but I can't see what's inside. She keeps walking and after a moment, she is out of sight. A few minutes later, though, she is back.

"There's a room with two sets of bunk beds and a twin bed. Who wants the twin?" she reports.

"Talia, you take it. If that's ok with everyone else," JJ says.

We all nod.

"Yeah, Talia, you can take it," Carter adds.

"Ok," Talia says.

She whispers something to JJ and then heads off to bed. Zoë follows. Carter and I both get up to go, but I notice that JJ stays seated.

"Aren't you tired?" I ask.

"I'm completely exhausted, but Talia and I are going to take shifts. Just in case. We just think that someone should be awake at all times ... just to be safe," he explains.

"Oh okay," I reply.

I head down the dimly lit hallway, pushing open the second door. Inside, it is completely empty, except for a gray desk and chair. Closing the door, I head farther down the hallway. When I push open the fourth door, I see the bedroom Talia described. Talia is asleep on the twin bed, her blonde hair spread out on the pillow. Zoë is on the top of the bunk on the left side of the room, and Carter is on the top bunk on the right. Going over to Zoë's bunk bed, I collapse on the bottom bunk, falling asleep the moment my head hits the pillow.

* * *

Someone is shaking me. I open my eyes and see Talia leaning over me.

"I know it's the middle of the night, but I'm so tired. Sometimes magic can really drain you. Can you finish my shift for me?" she begs.

"Sure," I reply.

I tiptoe out of the room and sit down on a metal bench in the main sitting area where we were hanging out earlier. I buckle the seatbelt. Have you ever slept in a bed with a seatbelt on it? I must say, it was quite uncomfortable. I know it's for safety reasons, but still.

I shiver, my mind drifting to Artemis. My eyes brim with tears, thinking of my little sister in some dark corner somewhere, alone and scared. That is if she is even still alive. If she's gone ... I don't know what I'll do.

"I'll find you, Artemis. I promise," I whisper, my voice shaking, tiny raindrop-like tears beginning to fall.

"Talia?" whispers a voice suddenly, causing me to nearly jump out of my skin.

I reply, "Talia's asleep. Who is that?"

"Carter," the voice says.

He comes out of the doorway of the room and sits down next to me on the bench.

"Did I wake you?" I ask, butterflies forming in my stomach.

"No...well yes," he says.

"Sorry."

"It's okay."

He looks at me and seems to notice my cheeks wet with tears, my eyes rimmed with red.

"Are you all right?" he asks, his forehead wrinkling with worry.

"I'm fine," I tell him quickly.

Carter raises his eyebrows skeptically. "Are you sure?"

"Yes. It's just ... I-I miss my sister. I don't even know if she's still alive, and ... well ... " I pause, struggling to find the words to convey how I'm feeling.

Carter puts his arm around me comfortingly. For a moment, I stiffen up, unsure how to react. But then, after a couple more seconds, I relax into the comfort of his embrace.

"I...I failed her, Carter. I shouldn't have let them take her away. I should have stopped them," I sniffle.

"You're going to find her, Alavis," he assures me.

"You don't know that!" I cry, pulling away from him.

"We'll find her."

"How can you be so sure?" I demand, my voice breaking.

He doesn't respond.

I drop my head into my hands, squeezing my eyes shut to keep the tears back. "The world is so unfair sometimes."

Carter is silent and for a moment, I'm worried that he's left. But when I open my eyes again, he is looking at me thoughtfully.

He says, "I agree. If only we could all have happily ever afters. I think we deserve it after all of the hardships we've all been through."

"We do deserve a happily ever after. But unfortunately, those who deserve a happy ending never seem to get one," I sigh.

Chapter 12

We spent the next few days just hanging out and having fun. I've never felt more relaxed. I finally have friends. You don't really make too many friends living on the streets. You're all too busy fighting to get the best sleeping spot or the best leftovers at a restaurant. And at the Marden, you're all locked up. You don't get to just hang out and have fun.

Two days ago, we started teaching Zoë how to read. There are no schools on Caldoria for magic kids, but my parents taught me to read, write, and all of the other things the non-magic kids learn in school. And yesterday, we all played charades after dinner. Carter was on my team, and we failed miserably, but it was still really fun. We played hide and seek around the ship, too, which was great until we couldn't find Zoë anywhere. Turns out she had decided to turn invisible, which is why we couldn't find her. When she finally appeared out of thin air, Carter nearly jumped out of his skin. It was hilarious.

"Alavis, hurry up!" shouts Talia, snapping me out of my thoughts.

I quickly finish brushing my long, wavy, dark blue hair. Before you ask, it's not dyed. Some people try to dye their hair this color, but mine is natural. I put the brush down, and look at myself in the mirror. My eyes are dark gray, and despite the brushing, my hair is still slightly knotty. I'm about to pick up the brush again when I hear a loud sigh from the hallway.

"You've been in there for 30 minutes already! The rest of us need to get ready!" Talia groans, knocking on the bathroom door for the millionth time.

"She wants to look good for Carter," JJ laughs.

I swing open the door, and it nearly hits both of them in the face. I quickly survey the hallway. Phew, Carter isn't out there. Not that it would matter or anything, since I don't like him. Well I mean, of course, I like him, but I don't like like him.

"Alavis, you've got a line out here. You take forever. Tomorrow, you're getting ready last," says Talia.

She goes into the bathroom and shuts the door. JJ and Zoë are both waiting to go in and get ready.

"JJ, next comment you make … " I warn, forming a fireball.

"I'm deeply sorry. You're boyfri— I mean friend is in the cockpit, in case you're wondering," he says, suppressing a smile.

"I wasn't wondering," I snap.

I wish he would stop teasing me. I don't like Carter! I walk down the hallway and sit down in one of the seats. I buckle my seatbelt. Talia said we should wear a seatbelt whenever we can. There's even a seatbelt on the toilet. Weird, I know. A moment later, Carter emerges from the cockpit.

"How's Zoë's magical aviator doing?" I ask.

He shrugs. "Good. I asked it when we'll get there, but it didn't respond."

"Maybe it only answers to Zoë," I suggest.

"Or maybe it just doesn't talk. I guess the ship will just stop when we get there," Carter says, clearly unsure.

"Breakfast, anyone?" asks Talia, walking into the room.

The ship was stocked with a couple months worth of food, hygiene products (toothbrushes, toothpaste, hairbrushes, etc.), and lots of clothes when we got on it. I wonder if this is one of the ships that the Marden uses to take people away. Artemis could have been taken away on a ship just like this. I take a deep breath, smoothing the wrinkles out of the t-shirt I am wearing today. It is black with the words: **CALDORIA SPACE TRAVELERS** on it, and I paired it with a pair of dark blue jeans. It's not the most fashionable outfit, but it's what was on the ship. And honestly, anything's better than the gray Marden jumpsuit. Imagine having to wear the same outfit for 5 years.

"Alavis, are you coming?" Talia says.

I get up, and we head to the spaceship's kitchen. The metallic gray table is barely big enough for all of us to sit around. Once we are all seated, though, we fasten our seatbelts.

"Okay, breakfast is served," Talia announces a few minutes later, setting a plate of bread and eggs on the table.

Carter, Talia, and I start eating, and after five minutes, JJ joins us. Five more minutes pass, and then Zoë arrives.

"Talia, can you pass me a piece of bread?" I ask.

She tosses it to me, and I reach out to catch it, completely missing. It falls to the floor.

"Wow, Alavis. Good job," Talia laughs.

I roll my eyes at her, and her face suddenly turns serious.

"Alavis, I wanted to tell you something," she says.

"What's up?" I ask.

"I wanted to say that I'm sorry I said you slowed us down during the escape. I mean you did, but you also helped us. You're a lot more powerful and strong than most people without any training would be," she says, not making eye contact with me.

"It's okay, Talia, really. But I appreciate your apology. Thank you," I reply.

"I don't have training, and I can make magic figures, freeze things, shapeshift, and turn invisible," Zoë points out.

"Maybe you're special like Alavis," Talia says to her.

Zoë smiles.

"I wish I had cool powers like that. But I guess I'm not special like Alavis and Zoë are," Carter sighs.

"You're smarter than all of us combined. That's something," I offer.

He just shrugs, as if dismissing what I said.

The Prisoner of Cell 47

"What decides what powers you have?" Zoë asks.

"It depends what your parents' powers were. You usually have a combination of their powers," Talia explains.

Zoë looks around at each of us. "What powers do you all have?"

"I have invisibility, telekinesis, shapeshifting, and the ability to create force fields. I may have more that I haven't discovered yet though," Talia says.

"I can walk through walls, and I have x-ray vision, but I don't know what my other powers are," JJ says.

"How come Talia knows more of her powers?" Zoë inquires, her bright green eyes filled with curiosity.

JJ grins. "I don't know. She's definitely way more powerful and much better at magic than I am. That's probably why."

Talia blushes.

"Alavis, what are your powers?" says Zoë.

"The ones I know so far are fire, telekinesis, and invisibility," I tell her.

"Fire's cool. Carter, what about you?" Zoë continues.

"Um.. I don't really know any of mine yet ... " he mumbles, looking at the floor.

85

"Hey, don't be embarrassed. JJ and I only know ours because we're older. And Alavis and Zoë...well I think they're just unusually powerful. JJ only discovered his first power when he was 15," Talia says.

Carter replies, "I'm 15."

"It'll be fine, Carter. You'll discover a power soon," says JJ.

Zoë taps her chin thoughtfully. "Is being super smart a power?"

"Maybe. We don't know if he's just very smart, or if he has the power of super intelligence," shrugs Talia.

"Here I am, on a ship with all these powerful, strong, great magic kids, and all I have is being smart," Carter sighs.

He gets up and walks away.

Chapter 13

Carter spent most of the day locked up in the bedroom. We're about to have dinner, but I don't think he'll come. I feel really bad for him. It makes sense for JJ and Talia to know a lot of their powers since they're 17, but I'm a year younger than Carter, and I know 3 of my powers already. And Zoë is only 6 years old! She's discovered more of her powers than I have. I didn't discover my first power until I was two years older than Zoë is now.

Back in the Marden, we couldn't really interact with the other people. I mean, sometimes, I would talk to a kid for a minute while I was in line for the shower, but that was kind of it. Anyway, I never really knew how many powers each person had discovered. I just assumed that it was normal for someone my age to know a couple of their powers. Maybe Talia's right. Maybe I am special.

"Can someone go ask Carter if he's joining us for dinner?" asks JJ.

"Alavis, go ask him," Talia orders.

My cheeks turn red. "Why me?"

"Because I don't feel like it," she shrugs.

I sigh, but get up. I head to the bedroom and knock on the door.

"Come in," he says.

"It's sort of locked."

"Oh." I hear footsteps, and a moment later, the door swings open.

"JJ wanted me to ask if you're going to have dinner with us," I tell him, leaning against the doorframe.

"Why wouldn't I?" he responds, his voice cold.

"Because you skipped lunch, and have been sitting in the room all day," I remind him.

He doesn't say anything.

"So, you're coming?" I clarify.

He is silent again for a moment, but then he shrugs. "Yeah, sure."

I want to comfort him, but I really don't know what to say to make him feel better.

"Carter, it's … well … " I cut off, thinking for a moment before continuing. "It's… it's okay not to know your powers. You don't have to be embarrassed."

"The average age to begin to discover your powers is 13-15. I'm 15, and I haven't discovered any of mine yet. I think that's reason to be embarrassed," he snaps.

"You'll discover one. I know you will," I tell him gently.

He scowls. "How do you know? Can you see into the future?"

"Hey, don't be mad at me! I'm trying to make you feel better!" I exclaim.

"You can't make me feel better! Everything worked out perfectly for you. You got your powers even earlier than most people, so you don't get to pretend you understand."

"Everything did not work out perfectly for me just because I got my powers early. My life is far from perfect. My parents are dead, I don't know where my sister is, I've been locked u—"

"I'm sorry, Alavis. I didn't mean that. It's just ... I ..." Carter mumbles, looking at the floor. "I may not get powers at all."

"What are you talking about?"

"My mom was magic. So was my sister," Carter says, his eyes glued to the floor. "But my dad ... he didn't have magic."

"You mean your dad was a non-magic?" I clarify.

"Yeah. So, I could be non-magic too. That's why I'm so scared that my powers haven't shown up yet."

"But why does it matter if you're non-magic?"

"Because I feel like I'm letting my family down if I don't have magic. And, I'm all alone, Alavis. My family is gone. And magic is a way for me to feel connected to my mom and sister, even though they're not around anymore."

"Cart—"

"Alavis, you can't tell the others," he interrupts.

"Why not?"

"Because ... I'm scared. If I don't have magic, what if they don't let me escape with them anymore? I mean, even if I don't have magic, I still want to leave Caldoria. And, what if they don't trust me anymore?"

"Carter, that's not going to happen. It'll—"

"Alavis. Please don't tell them. Just give me a little more time to discover a power," he pleads, his eyes wide.

"I promise I won't tell them," I reply. "But Carter, I—"

Carter's face changes from anxious to angry again.

"Alavis, whatever you're about to say, stop. I don't want to hear about how if I just believe, it'll all be ok. I'll get my powers, and it will all be great. I have no clue what's going to happen, Alavis, and that terrifies me!" he snaps, his brown eyes filled with bitterness.

He pushes past me and heads towards the kitchen. I wait a minute, annoyed at his reaction. I was being nice and trying to comfort him. I didn't deserve to be yelled at. But still, I wish I could have said something better. Something that would have helped him. With a sigh, I walk over to Talia, JJ, and Zoë.

"What happened?" Talia asks.

"I don't want to talk about it," I reply frustratedly.

"Okay. We're about to go into the kitchen to have dinner," Talia says.

"Let's go. I'm hungry," JJ adds, and Zoë whines, "Me too."

We head to the kitchen and see Carter already sitting down at the table. There is a plate of chicken and potatoes in front of him.

"I've been waiting here for forever. What took so long?" he asks.

"You've been waiting two seconds," JJ replies.

"Whatever," mumbles Carter.

"Let's eat. I'm starving," says Talia, trying to change the subject.

We start eating, and I end up sitting right across from Carter. After a few minutes of awkward silence, Carter says that he's sorry for staying shut up in the room all day.

"And Alavis, I'm sorry I snapped at you," he adds.

"It's okay."

We all eat in awkward silence for the next couple minutes. I start thinking about Artemis again. Where could she be?

"Someone on Masthinya must know," I say.

"Huh?" Talia replies.

"Someone there must know where all the people that were taken from the Marden are, right?" I say, hoping I am right.

JJ sighs. "How would someone on Masthinya know? They may not even know what the Marden is."

"I guess you're probably right. But you think they have some sort of magic that they can use to find Artemis, right?" I ask.

"Let's hope."

* * *

The next day, Carter calls all of us into the cockpit. When we come in, he is standing over an electronic map labeled "Masthinya."

"We need a specific place to land the ship. But, we don't know any of the places ... so where do we set our course for?" Carter explains.

He zooms in and starts reading off names of places.

"Ahiata, Ceranae, Traversa, Bavlore, Del—"

"Wait. I recognize the name Bavlore," I say, surprised.

I've definitely seen the name before, but I can't recall where I've seen it. I close my eyes, trying to think. And then suddenly, it comes back to me.

My mom is standing next to me, her long blue locks falling into her eyes. She is wearing her favorite jacket, the gray raincoat that my dad got for her. Sticking out of her pocket, like always, is a map. The label on the map says "Bavlore."

"My mom. She always carried a map of Bavlore with her," I say to my friends.

"Why?" Talia asks.

"I don't know."

JJ shrugs. "It doesn't really matter why. It's a place we've heard of at least, so I say we set our course for there."

Carter nods in agreement and clicks a couple of buttons on the screen.

A robotic voice states, "Setting course for Bavlore."

"Okay. That's settled. So ... lunch?" JJ asks.

Chapter 14

A bout a week or two later, I see a planet coming into view. It is a magnificent swirl of different shades of pink, orange, and red.

"Guys! Come here!" I cry.

Everyone rushes to the cockpit.

"We're so close," says Talia excitedly.

"Zoë, can you ask your magic aviator when we'll arrive?" Carter asks.

"I don't know if it will answer, but I'll try," she responds.

"What is our arrival time?" Zoë asks the aviator.

No response.

"Arrival time, please," she repeats.

The aviator just keeps flying the ship. Zoë closes her eyes.

"What is our arrival time?" she mumbles. She waves her hand in the air, and the aviator glows brightly.

A voice echoes around the room: **"Hello, Zoë and companions. You will be arriving in approximately one day."**

"One day?!" I squeal excitedly.

My excitement is quickly replaced by guilt, and I almost feel sick to my stomach. How can I feel excitement when I haven't found Artemis yet? I take a deep breath. *The people of Masthinya will be able to find her. They'll use their magic and find her. And if they don't, I'll find her on my own.*

"We should pack," says Talia, pulling me out of my thoughts.

She runs off down the hallway, and returns with bags for each of us. I head to the bedroom and open my bag. I throw in a bunch of clothes and a bunch of toiletries from the bathroom. I grab a couple snacks from the kitchen, and zip the bag shut. Sitting down, I wait for the others to finish. Zoë comes to sit down next to me a couple minutes later.

"Hey Zo. Are you excited to get to Masthinya?" I ask her.

"Yeah. Are we all going to live together?" she replies.

"Huh. I didn't really think about where we would live. All I've been thinking about is finding Artemis. I haven't thought about where I'll live after I find her," I say.

Zoë's wide green eyes fill with fear. "Don't leave me alone, please."

"Oh Zoë, I would never leave you," I promise her.

"Really?" she says, her lower lip trembling.

"Really."

Zoë smiles, and pushes her hair out of her face.

"Do you want me to put your hair up for you?" I offer.

"Okay," she says happily.

I go to the bathroom and find two hair ties. I come back and put Zoë's curly red hair into two buns. She goes to look in the mirror.

"Do you like it?" I ask, once she's back.

"Yes. You're like the big sister I never had," she tells me.

I give her a hug.

"Do you miss your sister?" Zoë asks me suddenly.

"I miss her so much. I haven't seen her in a year," I reply, a tear rolling down my cheek.

"We'll find her. Don't worry," says Zoë reassuringly.

"Thanks, Zoë."

Everyone finishes packing, and we all sit together on the cold metal chairs in the main sitting area.

"Where are we going to stay?" I ask.

Talia shrugs. "We'll figure it out."

"When?" I demand.

"We'll ask someone if we can stay with them. We'll only be there for a few days anyway, and then we're setting out to find your sister," Talia suggests.

"A stranger is going to let five random people stay in their house. Sure. Sounds like a plan," laughs JJ.

"Well, we'll need somewhere to live after we find Artemis," I continue, ignoring JJ's comment.

"We'll figure it out," Talia repeats.

Chapter 15

W e're here. We're actually here. The ship landed ten minutes ago, and we're actually, actually here. None of us have moved yet. We've all just stood here for the last ten minutes taking everything in. The area we landed in is a large grassy field dotted with yellow flowers. Off in the distance, I see rolling hills, and beyond that, I can just make out the outline of a village. Brightstar is beginning to set, and I feel like I could just sit in the grass and stare at this view forever.

"Guys, we should really start walking. We need to find

somewhere to sleep tonight," Talia reminds us.

"Yeah," I sigh, picking my bag up off of the ground.

JJ and Talia walk ahead of the rest of us, holding hands, making their way through the tall grass towards the outline of the village.

"How long until we get to that village?" Zoë asks me.

"I don't know, Zo. I can carry you on my back if you get tired," I offer.

"I'm good for now. But thanks," she replies.

It's silent for a minute or two as we pass by tall green trees and butterflies fluttering through the field.

The silence is broken when Carter says, "Alavis, what if nobody lets us stay with them? I don't want to have to live on the streets again, even if it's only for a few days."

"I would say, 'we'll be fine', but I really don't know. We just have to hope for the best," I shrug, trying to hide my nervousness. I've been having the same worries.

"What are you guys talking about?" JJ asks as we catch up to him and Talia.

"We're just talking about how we don't want to end up on the streets again," Carter responds.

"You two need to lighten up. We made it to Masthinya! Be happy about that, and stop worrying," JJ says.

"There *are* important things to worry about, though," I point out.

"Yes, there are. But you should just enjoy the moment for now," JJ says with a laugh.

"Fine," I sigh, rolling my eyes.

"And anyway, we're only staying a few nights. After that, we search for your sister," JJ adds.

"What about when we get back?" Carter says.

Talia mutters, "If we get back."

"I didn't say you had to come! You offered!" I snap, my cheeks flushing.

Her comment makes me anxious though. If someone gets hurt, or worse, while we're looking for Artemis... will it be my fault because it's my sister they're looking for?

"Calm down guys. Seriou—" JJ starts.

Talia interjects. "Where's Zoë?"

We look around. Uh oh.

"Zoë?" I call out, starting to panic.

My heart beats loudly in my chest. Where is she?

"Meow." A kitten appears from behind a bush, and brushes against my leg.

I pick up the kitten. "Zoë, you scared us!"

The cat shapeshifts back into person form. "Sorry. Didn't mean to scare you."

"It's okay."

We keep walking, and I am in awe of the beauty of it all. I don't think I've ever seen a place this beautiful on Caldoria. Although I haven't really seen much of Caldoria. Still, Masthinya just looks so peaceful, with all the flowers and trees, and the orange and red sky as Brightstar sets. I wonder, hope filling my heart, if this could be somewhere that Artemis and I might someday call home.

"Are we almost there?" asks Zoë.

"I don't know, but I hope so. I'm tired," I reply.

* * *

Finally, a few hours later, we arrive at the village. We pass what appears to be the town square, encircled by a variety of small shops, and we keep walking down a long dirt road. Since it's late, nobody is out.

"So, do we just knock on people's doors?" I say.

"I guess," Carter shrugs.

A street of cozy-looking houses comes into view. The houses are all small and cottage-like, with potted plants by the windows, and we knock on the first couple doors. Nobody responds. When we knock on the door of a forest green-colored house, a tall woman with short, curly, dark purple hair answers the door.

"Do you kids need something?" she asks.

JJ nudges Zoë forward. Smart move. People have a harder time saying no to a little kid.

"We're ... uh ... new here, and we were wondering ... if you had an extra room or something. It's just, we don't have anywhere to sleep ... if we could just spend one night ... please," Zoë says.

It sounds as if she's about to start crying. The woman stares at us.

"Do you have magic?" she inquires, and we nod.

"Come inside. Now. It's not safe for you to be roaming about the village alone," the woman says urgently, peering anxiously down the street.

We go inside, and she locks the door behind us. Talia gives me a nervous look as we enter the brightly lit foyer, the floorboards creaking beneath our feet. The house is very warm and comforting, especially compared to the shabby little apartment my family used to live in. It belonged to a non-magic woman, but she was one of the very few who didn't despise magic people, so she let us stay there. But that apartment looked nothing like this place. Peering down the hallway, I see a living room, with a fireplace, and a big plush sofa. The apartment never had anything like that. Or even any comfortable furniture for that matter. But it was a roof over our heads and that was all that mattered. That is until the woman who owned the apartment died, and that roof over our heads was gone.

I hear a soft murmuring noise and glance over in Talia's direction.

She is muttering to herself, "We shouldn't have come inside. We don't know if we can trust her. What was I thinking? I should have said 'no, we won't come inside until we know you're someone we can trust ...'"

The woman hears her.

"I'm sorry if I made you feel nervous. I only locked the door because it is unsafe out in the village for you children," the woman explains, pulling down the shades.

"Why is it unsafe?" I ask worriedly.

"Nobody can know you're here. They will come, and try to

take your magic," replies the woman, guiding us into the living room.

"Who?" demands Talia, confused.

"The townsfolk."

"Why?" says Carter, his attention drifting towards the pile of books and magazines on the table. He picks one up and sits down on the couch, starting to glance through the pages.

"Because the Elvaquins came and took our magic about a week ago, and now the townsfolk are so bitter that they will be mad that you all have magic. Now, where are you kids from?" the woman asks.

"Why should we tell you?" snaps Talia.

"Wait, the Elvaquins? Like people from the planet of Elvaqua?" adds JJ, flopping down on the couch.

The woman doesn't respond to either of them and instead walks over to me. She studies my face thoughtfully, her gaze fixing on my hair.

"You look just like— I mean, I haven't seen hair that color since ... " She stops. "You're Penny's daughter."

Chapter 16

"You knew my mom?" I ask.

The woman nods shakily, and holds out her hand. "I'm Joy Peterson. Your mother was my best friend."

I shake her hand. "Alavis Hansen. We're from the planet Caldoria."

"Alavis! Why would you tell her that?" Talia hisses, her cheeks flushing with anger.

"She knew my mom!"

"That doesn't mean we can trust her!" Talia shouts, pounding her fist against the couch cushion.

"Yes, it does," I snap, a wall of fury blinding my common sense.

Doesn't Talia care that I've found someone who knew my mom?

"Alavis, where is your mother? And your father?" Joy asks me.

"I think ... they're dead ... I mean I don't know for sure, but I always assumed. They left one day and never came back."

Tears form in my eyes, and Joy hugs me.

"Maybe they just abandoned you," Talia mumbles under her breath.

I whirl around to face her. "Hey! My parents would never abandon Artemis and me! They left to help us. To give us a better life. Take that back, Talia. Now," I cry, my body shaking with anger.

"I'll take it back if you stop giving our secrets away to a woman we just met!" responds Talia, her eyes challenging.

"Talia, what's gotten into you?" JJ asks.

I form a fireball.

"Woah, Alavis, put the fire away," Carter says, getting up from the couch.

"No. Not until she takes back what she said," I reply.

Talia shapeshifts into a lion, knocking over a small table in the process, and roars loudly.

She could be right. Maybe they are alive. Maybe they didn't leave for us. Maybe they just didn't want us, I think to myself. No. I won't believe that. The ball of fire in my palm grows larger. Zoë starts to cry, and Joy picks her up, backing away from Talia and me.

"It's okay, honey. Don't cry. They won't hurt each other," Joy whispers soothingly. She glances at us disapprovingly. "Both of you, stop this. You nee—"

Talia roars again, cutting Joy off.

JJ gets up from the couch and walks over to the golden lion that Talia has turned into. He kneels down next to her, saying something I can't hear, to try to calm her down. Carter comes over to me cautiously.

"Alavis, put the fire away," he says placatingly.

"No."

"Alavis ... "

"No."

Carter sighs exasperatedly. "She didn't mean what she said."

"Yes, she did."

"She was just upset. You'll never forgive yourself if you hurt her," he says.

The fire in my hand shrinks a little bit. "She needs to

apologize. A real apology. Then, I won't burn her with fire," I say.

Carter runs over to JJ, and tells him this. He tells Talia, who is back in human form. She nods, not making eye contact.

"Alavis, I'm really, truly sorry. I don't know what came over me. I'm sure your parents didn't abandon you. I'm sure everything you said about them leaving for you is true. I was just upset, because I didn't know if we could trust Joy. I'm sorry for what I said, and I'm sorry for not trusting your judgment. Please, please, please forgive me," Talia says, finally making eye contact with me.

Her apology feels genuine.

"I won't say it's okay, because it's not, but I'll forgive you, I guess," I sigh.

She comes over and tries to give me a hug. I back away.

"I need to be alone."

* * *

Joy had multiple extra rooms, so we each got our own bedroom. I've been lying in bed for the past four hours, staring at the clouds painted onto the pale blue ceiling, trying to fall asleep. Talia's words keep replaying in my head.

Maybe they just abandoned you. Maybe they just abandoned

you ... abandoned you ... abandoned ... abandoned ...

Why did I never look for them? I mean, I was young, and spending each day trying to keep my sister and I fed and alive. I didn't have time to look! But still ... I should have. The thing is, Talia only voiced a thought that has gone through my head a million times before. I mean, did my parents truly leave to find a better life for Artemis and me? Or did they just leave? And how can I ever really know? I sigh, burying my face in my pillow. Suddenly, there is a knock on the door.

"Who is it?" I ask.

"Joy."

"Come in," I say, my voice muffled from the pillow.

With another sigh, I sit up. I don't feel like talking to anyone, but Joy is giving us a place to stay, so I don't want to be rude. Once the door is open all the way, she walks in.

"How are you?" she says.

"Not great," I reply truthfully.

Joy nods sympathetically, and sits down in a wooden rocking chair in the corner of the room. "I think that your parents knew, Alavis," states Joy.

"Knew what?" I ask, feeling kind of annoyed, waiting for her to elaborate.

"I think that they knew, somehow, about the Elvaquins' plan. Maybe because your father, Lance, was Elvaquin. Anyway—"

"My father was from Elvaqua?" I say, cutting her off.

She raises her eyebrows in surprise. "You didn't know that?"

"Nope. Up until today, I thought that both of my parents were from Caldoria," I tell her.

"That's odd. I wonder why Penny and Lance never told you," Joy says.

I can feel my anger starting to build up. Why didn't my parents ever tell me anything about them? Didn't they care about me at all? I take a few deep breaths, trying not to let my anger get the best of me.

"But wait, isn't Elvaqua the worst planet?" I ask her, trying to move my mind onto other subjects.

"What exactly do you mean by worst?" Joy replies.

"I-I don't know ... Talia said that the person who taught her and JJ said Elvaqua was the worst planet," I shrug.

"Well, the people in power in Elvaqua are quite evil, in my opinion. I think everyone in this village, and on Masthinya, would agree."

111

"Joy, what happened? What did the Elvaquins do?" I say curiously, twisting a strand of my dark blue hair around my finger.

Joy sighs. "It was just a normal day. I went into the bakery to pick something up, and when I came back out, the square was filled with Elvaquin guards. Now, Masthinya does have an army, but their bases were attacked right when the Elvaquins came. Our army was taken by surprise. Every Elvaquin guard had a tall mahogany staff. At the top, there was an Althenian crystal—"

"What is an Althenian crystal?" I inquire, stopping her.

"It's a very rare, magical crystal. And the guards used their magic staffs to take all our magic. They just pointed the staff at us, and our magic was drained. It was like ... like a part of me was being taken away. It was awful." She pauses, taking a deep breath. "Anyway, the magic went into the crystal, I think. Everyone in Masthinya was weak for days. Some people still haven't recovered. I still don't understand why they took our magic," she says.

"Power," I guess bitterly. "They probably just wanted more power."

"You're probably right, Alavis," Joy replies with a dejected sigh.

"What about my parents?" I ask, desperate for any information on them.

"They had left long ago. I said earlier that I think they knew the Elvaquins would do this, so they left. Your mother, Penny, was pregnant with you at the time. They didn't give an explanation when they left, so I'm just thinking now that they must have known about the Elvaquins' plan. Anyway, I was so sad that my best friend was leaving and that I would never get to meet her child. I'm so glad I'm meeting you now, Alavis," Joy says, her face brightening.

"I'm glad to meet you too. Joy, can you tell me anything about my parents' personalities ... or what they liked ... or anything? I don't know anything about them," I beg.

Joy is quiet for a moment.

"Your mother was extremely kind and caring. I remember that she had the most contagious laugh. She did have a bit of a temper, though. Seems like you got that from her," Joy says with a chuckle.

I smile, knowing that I have some connection to my mom. Suddenly, Joy's face turns serious.

"Alavis ... this temper is something you should be very careful with. It created many problems for your mother. I ... just ... be careful, Alavis."

"I will," I promise, unsure what kind of problems she means, and then quickly change the subject. "What can you tell me about my father?"

"I didn't know him very well. He was quiet and intelligent. Always seemed to be reading or writing something. He loved Penny very much. That's all I really know, Alavis."

"Joy, you were best friends with my mother. You knew her well. Do you believe that if she left Artemis and me, she did it for us? To find us a better life?" I murmur hopefully.

"I do, Alavis. I truly do."

"And do you think that maybe, when my parents left Caldoria, they were coming back to Masthinya? If they knew that the Elvaquins would do this, maybe they felt bad and came back to check that everyone was alright? Maybe they wanted to help fix things here so that we could all come live here," I ask. Joy's face darkens.

"If they did, then they would be here, wouldn't they?"

ChaptER 17

⁓

"I don't have anything in the house I'm afraid. I usually eat breakfast at the diner," Joy tells us the next morning, searching through the kitchen pantries.

"That's fine. We can go to the diner," I shrug.

"We're not picky," JJ adds, sitting down across from me at the little breakfast nook.

Joy shakes her head. "I'll just run to the diner and pick something up."

"Why can't we go?" Zoë asks, as I braid her hair.

"Because the townsfolk will know you have magic. They're all depressed and longing for their magic. They'll try to steal yours. Some of them will do whatever it takes. And if they can't figure out how to steal your magic, well ... I'm not sure what they'll do ... but things could turn violent," Joy explains anxiously.

Zoë's eyes fill with fear.

"Are they going to hurt us?" she trembles.

I pull Zoë onto my lap.

"Don't worry, Zo. We'll be safe," I say soothingly.

"You shouldn't lie to her," Joy tells me with a sigh.

"She's only six!" I cry.

Joy sighs again. "You're only putting her in danger. The less you know, the more vulnerable you are."

"Okay. Fine! Zoë, you're not safe. They might take your magic and attack you and kill you. There Joy, are you happy?!" I shout, storming out of the room.

I go into my bedroom and lock the door. I can still hear their voices, faintly, as I throw a vase at the wall. It shatters into a million little pieces, but this does nothing to lessen my anger.

"Someone go talk to her," I hear Joy say.

I'm sure that Joy just wants us to be safe, but a six-year-old shouldn't have to hear that her life is in danger! I just want a relaxing and safe life. Is that really so much to ask?

"I shouldn't go. She hates me," Talia mutters.

"She doesn't hate you, Talia. She's just upset at you, and I'm sure she'll get over it. So, who of us has the best chance of calming her down?" JJ asks.

"Why do we need to calm her down? Let's just give her some time," Talia grumbles.

"These people might try to steal our magic and attack us! We want everyone alert, ready, and calm," JJ says. "I'll comfort Zoë, and Carter you go talk to Alavis. She's likely to listen to you."

I hear footsteps, and then a knock on the door. I'm really not in the mood to talk, so I try to turn myself invisible. It works. I guess I've gotten stronger!

"Alavis? ...Alavis? ...Alavis, you there?"

There is a series of clicking noises, and a minute later, the door swings open. Carter stands in the doorway. He must have picked the lock. He is a super-genius, after all.

"Alavis? Are you okay?" he asks, his voice filled with concern.

I see him glance at the broken vase on the floor.

"Alavis?"

I don't respond, hoping he'll just leave. He doesn't. He takes a step into the room, and then he screams. I immediately turn visible and run over to him.

"Carter, are you alright?" I ask nervously.

He stares at the closet next to the bed, his eyes wide.

"Carter? You okay?" I repeat.

"D-do … do you see it?" he stutters, looking at me desperately.

"See what?" I reply.

He points at the closet.

"I … I see inside of the closet … but it's closed. I see the clothes inside … Alavis, why can I see the clothes inside?!" he says, nearly shouting.

I put my hand on his shoulder.

"Calm down," I tell him. "I think I may know what's going on."

I rush out of the room to find JJ. I see him sitting on the couch, Zoë on his lap.

"JJ, you said you have x-ray vision, right?" I ask quickly, and he nods.

"Come quick."

I run back to the room, and Carter is still staring at the closet, shaking.

"I...I see the inside, Alavis ... the inside ... ," he murmurs, pressing his hands to his head. "Please, make it stop. Make it stop!"

JJ walks through the wall a moment later. Can't he just use the door? I mean it's a cool power, but it's really strange to see someone walk through a wall.

"What's wrong?" JJ inquires.

"He keeps saying that he can see what's inside the closet, even though it's closed," I explain.

JJ smiles and pats Carter on the back. "You've got x-ray vision, kid."

Chapter 18

I was expecting Carter to be excited, but instead, he looks like he's about to throw up.

"It's everywhere, JJ. I see inside everything. How do I make it go away?" he cries, pacing back and forth. "The drawers, the closet, the box of books by the wall … it's like they're all open … but they're not … "

"It's okay, Carter. You just have to learn to control it. Take a deep breath," JJ responds.

Carter stops pacing and takes a deep breath.

"Now, imagine your x-ray vision as an object," JJ instructs.

"Huh? How can x-ray vision be an object?" I ask, my brows furrowing in confusion.

"Shut up, Alavis. I'm trying to help him here," JJ grumbles, glaring at me.

"Rude," I mutter sarcastically.

JJ scowls at me.

"Okay, okay, I'll be quiet."

"So, Carter, imagine the x-ray vision as an object. Now imagine a box. I want you to open the box, put the object in, and shut the box. Lock it. Whenever you need your x-ray vision, just open the box and take it out. That's what I always imagine," JJ says.

Carter closes his eyes. "Put the x-ray in a box...lock it up ... " he murmurs. He opens his eyes, blinking a couple times, and looks around. "It's gone. Thanks, JJ. Sorry for freaking out," Carter says.

"No worries," JJ replies good-naturedly.

"Oh, I forgot. Alavis, you okay?" Carter asks suddenly.

"Huh?"

"I came in here to ask if you were okay," he explains.

"Oh yeah, I'm fine," I say quickly.

My anger almost entirely subsided while I was worrying

about Carter.

"I'm going to go tell the others that everything's fine," JJ says as he walks through the wall again.

Once JJ is gone, I smile at Carter. "Looks like you do have magic after all."

"Yeah. I'm sorry I freaked out about all of that to you," he says sheepishly.

"Don't worry about it," I reply. "I'm really happy for you, Carter."

A second later, Joy rushes into the room, Talia, JJ, and Zoë right behind her.

"They're here!" Joy cries with an alarmed tone.

My heart skips a beat.

"The Elvaquins?!" I exclaim, my pulse quickening as I start to panic. "No. My book club!" Joy replies, as if that is the most obvious thing ever.

JJ laughs. "Wait, Joy, your book club? So what?"

"They'll try to steal your magic!" Joy says.

"We'll hide while they're here," I suggest, opening the closet to see if there is enough room to fit all of us.

Joy looks at me thoughtfully. "Do you kids plan to stay here?"

she asks, her voice becoming calmer all of sudden.

"What do you mean?" I respond.

"You kids want to live on Masthinya right?"

"Well, first we're going to search for my sister, but when we find her, yes! Although I guess we could go to Zathen or Denima," I shrug.

"No. There are Mardens there too," JJ says.

"How do you know?" I demand.

"Because when I was living on the streets, I saw a kid getting dragged off to the Marden. I heard the guards talking. One said, 'This kid thought he could escape the Marden on Zathen and fly a spaceship here!' And the other laughed and said, 'How could he know that there's a Marden on Caldoria too!' And then the first guard said to the kid, 'Hey kid, there's a Marden on Denima too, so don't get any ideas.' The kid said, 'What's Denima? And what's Caldoria?' The guards laughed at him. I felt bad for the kid. How was he supposed to know about the different planets? They don't teach you that in the Marden. Anyway, then the guard said—"

I cut him off. "Okay, thanks JJ. I got it."

There's an awkward silence.

"Well, I don't think we can live on Camden with the animals.

And we're not going to Elvaqua. So, yes Joy, we want to live on Masthinya," I say finally.

"Took you long enough. I needed a quick yes or no, not a whole storytime. Anyway, you'll have to face the townsfolk eventually, so why not now?" Joy says. Her eye twitches nervously. "It'll be fine."

"How would they go about taking our magic? Just curious," JJ asks nervously.

"Hmm...I'm not sure. Now that I think about it, I don't think anyone on Masthinya has the magic staffs that the Elvaquins had. You should be fine. Although, they may just try to kill you, because they're jealous that you have magic," Joy tells us.

"Lovely," JJ replies.

"Wouldn't that make them just as bad as the Elvaquins?" I point out.

"Yes. Yes, it would. Now, let's go out and say hello. Try not to get killed," says Joy.

Chapter 19

"The only people I think you have to worry about are Lizzie and Logan Donsmith, Jack Andrews, Saria Elson, and Kiara Davis. Don't stress about anyone else trying to hurt you. The people I just named are all very jealous types and have all been moping about for weeks. Saria punched a guy in the face just for mentioning how sad it was that we don't have magic anymore," Joy whispers to us as we enter the living room.

Zoë's eyes are wide and innocent. "Why are they in your book club then, if they're jealous and mean?"

"Sit down, and smile. Don't mention the fact that you have magic," Joy orders, ignoring Zoë, and heading to the door.

"Well, duh," I mutter.

Joy glares at me. "This is serious, Alavis."

She opens the door, and members of her book club come pouring inside, greeting each other. Once everyone has arrived, we all sit down in the living room.

"Who are these children?" demands a woman with long midnight black hair. She's wearing a dark green dress and extremely tall high heels. Joy goes over to greet her.

"Saria, lovely to see you. How have yo—"

"Who are these children, Joy?" the woman, who must be Saria, repeats, giving us a menacing look.

"These are ... my cousin's children. I've got a cousin in Traversa, and he sadly passed away. His kids were sent to me," Joy lies.

Saria eyes us suspiciously.

"They are all related?" she asks, her eyebrows raised.

"Y-yes. Well, a few of them are adopted," Joy quickly says.

"Oh. What are their names? Will they be living in our village, Bavlore, or will you be moving all the way to Traversa, where your cousin is from?" Saria inquires.

"They will be going back to Traversa for a little bit, and then will be staying here. Oh, and they will introduce themselves," Joy replies, nodding at us.

"My name is Talia. Pleasure to meet you," says Talia politely.

"I'm JJ."

"I'm Alavis. Nice to meet you."

"Carter. Pleasure to meet you, Miss."

Zoë waves. "My name is Zoë."

"I'm Saria. Lizzie, Logan, come here! Meet the children. Kiara, Jack, Donna, Fran, Oliver, come over to me, and meet the children! Everyone, come. They will soon be living here with Joy," Saria calls out.

Everyone gathers around us. Joy looks nervous, beads of sweat dripping down her forehead.

"This is Talia, JJ, Alavis, Carter, and Zoë," Joy announces to the gathered people.

"Such adorable children!" one woman says.

Another woman adds, "Just darling!"

"Ok, now, let's have lunch, and then we will discuss the book," Joy says loudly.

"Oh, come on! We haven't even gotten to know the kids yet!" a woman with short, curly blonde hair whines, her hands on her hips.

"Oh Donna, you'll have plenty of time later. They'll be living here!" Joy replies, forcing a laugh.

Everyone enters the dining room, and Joy starts putting heaping trays of sandwiches, salads, and pastries on the long, wooden table. Zoë is sitting on my left, and Carter on my right. JJ is next to Zoë on the other side, and Talia is on the other side of Carter. The woman sitting across from us starts talking to us.

"I'm Lizzie. This is my husband Logan," she smiles.

"Nice to meet you," I reply.

Lizzie stares at me and then turns to Logan. "She looks just like Penny, doesn't she?" she asks him.

I glance at Joy frantically, but she is still bringing out the food and doesn't notice.

"And those eyes. Do you remember that man? The one who came on a spaceship, stayed here for three years, and then his parents found out that he was on Masthinya, and forced him to return home. Penny fell in love with him. Lance was his name, I think. He had gray eyes, just like the girl sitting across from us. Joy said her name was Alana?" Lizzie continues.

"Alavis, I believe," Logan responds, pouring himself a glass of water.

"Well anyway, Lance snuck back to Masthinya a few years later, and he and Penny got married. He was from Elvaqua, I think. What Penny saw in an Elvaquin, I don't know. They're all evil. But, they got married and then disappeared. That was years ago. They could have a kid Alana's age—"

"Alavis," Logan interjects.

"A kid Alavis' age. Joy!" Lizzie calls out.

Joy goes over to her. "Do you need something, Lizzie?" Joy asks.

"That girl. Alana. She has hair like Penny's and eyes like Lance. Yet you claim this is your cousin's child?" Lizzie demands.

Joy's face pales. "Yes. She's adopted."

"Hmm. I don't believe you. This here is a child of Penny and Lance. I'm sure of it," Lizzie tells Joy.

Lizzie pulls a sparkling silver dagger out of her boot and points it at me. "Where are you from?" she shouts.

The room goes silent.

"Lizzie, she's just a child. Put the dagger away!" cries Joy frantically.

"Where are you from?" Lizzie yells, walking around the table towards me.

My heart is racing. Do I tell her I'm from Caldoria? Do I use my magic to defend myself? I consider running, but I have a feeling Lizzie is fast. And if she's not, someone else will catch me. Maybe I could outrun them all though. Suddenly, she's in front of me, the dagger pointed at my chest. Too late for running now.

"Where are you from?" Lizzie growls, her hazel eyes filled with anger, pulling out a second dagger.

"Caldoria," I mutter, panicking.

"Caldoria. Interesting. I'm going to assume you're magic, or else why would you run from Caldoria. Do you have magic?" she asks.

"No," I lie.

"Saria," Lizzie says, handing her a dagger.

Saria nods, and pushes me against the wall, the dagger pointed at me. Out of the corner of my eye, I see that Joy is trying to get Talia, JJ, Zoë, and Carter out of the room, without Lizzie noticing. I watch as Carter points at me urgently. Joy motions for him to keep going.

"But—" he starts to say.

Lizzie hears the noise and turns in their direction. They start to bolt, but Lizzie is too fast.

Sprinting over to them, she manages to grab Zoë and then surveys the room. "Logan. Kiara. Jack. Get them."

Talia, JJ, and Carter stop running, glancing anxiously between the door, Zoë, and me.

"Just go!" I order.

They hesitate for another moment and then sprint out of the room. Logan, Kiara, and Jack are close on their tails.

"We don't have magic. Stop attacking us!" I snap as they race off, my palms starting to get warm.

I take a deep breath. I can't conjure fire right now if I'm trying to convince Saria that I don't have magic.

Saria glares at me, her face red with rage. "Our magic was stolen. It was taken from us by those wretched Elvaquins. Your father was an Elvaquin. And it is not fair for you kids to have magic when we don't!"

"I SAID WE DON'T HAVE MAGIC!" I scream, feeling the all too familiar anger beginning to break through the surface.

She growls, pressing her dagger against my neck. I wince as her blade draws blood.

"YOU'RE LYING! Why would you leave Caldoria if you didn't

have magic?! The non-magics have a good life there, do they not?" Saria scowls.

I take a deep breath, trying to keep my anger in check. But I just can't. I can't stop myself from yelling, "Don't you dare claim to know what it's like on Caldoria!"

"Excuse me?" Saria murmurs, warning in her voice.

"You have no idea what it's like there. You don't know what it was like to grow up there. I had no childhood. None worth reminiscing about anyway. And I thought that when I came to Masthinya, I would finally be welcomed. I would finally be somewhere where I didn't feel so alone. Where I didn't feel like the whole world was against me. And yet, here you are, attacking me because I have magic. Just like on Caldoria. I'm sorry your magic got taken, but that is not my fault, so don't you dare take it out on me!"

I quickly wipe my tears away, my face hot with fury. Saria stares at me, her expression softening slightly.

"She's gone!" Lizzie yells suddenly.

I glance over to see who Lizzie is talking about. I realize that she means Zoë. Zoë must have shapeshifted. A small bug scurrying on the floor catches my attention, confirming my suspicions.

"You were just trying to distract me. You, and your magic

---

friends," Saria snarls, hurling her dagger at the wall.

My heart skips a beat as the blade almost chops my ear off. In my peripheral vision, I can see the sparkling silver blade embedded in the wall next to me. I cannot die here. Not before I save Artemis.

Saria turns away for a moment to look for Zoë. While Saria is distracted, I turn myself invisible, sweating from the effort, and run out of the room.

"The blue-haired girl is gone!" I hear Saria exclaim in anger.

I burst out the front door. At that exact same moment, JJ runs through the wall and joins me outside. We duck behind a bush, trying to stay out of sight.

"Where's Talia? We need a forcefield!" JJ cries urgently.

"Weren't you with her?" I reply, worry seeping into my voice.

"We were being chased so we ended up getting split up!" he explains.

I can hear the panic in his voice.

"Uh oh," I say.

Logan and Lizzie swing open the front door and immediately spot us behind the bush. I guess that wasn't the best hiding spot. They run towards us. Lizzie hurls a dagger at me, and without thinking, I throw my hands forward, a huge gust of wind pushing

Logan and Lizzie backward into the house. The dagger flies off course and embeds itself in the dirt, and I then use my telekinesis to lock the door to the house.

"How's Talia going to get out?" JJ asks me.

Talia appears in front of the door. "I'll figure it out."

"You shapeshifted," JJ grins, giving her a kiss.

"Where's Zoë? And Carter?" I say worriedly.

Talia points at the door, "I don't know. But Logan and Lizzie are back."

I glance at the door, where Logan and Lizzie are now standing. Along with Saria and Jack.

"Alavis, do that wind thing again," JJ says.

"What wind thing?" Talia asks.

I thrust my hands forward. Nothing. I thrust them forward again, and a small gust of wind pushes Logan, Lizzie, Saria, and Jack back slightly.

"KIARA! GET OUT HERE! Show them what we have!" Lizzie yells, a smirk on her face.

Kiara opens the door, holding an unconscious Zoë in her arms.

"NO!" I cry, my heart pounding.

This is all my fault. I should have … I should have helped Zoë so that this didn't happen. Desperately, I throw my hands in front of me, and a huge gust of wind shoves them all to the ground. Zoë's eyes start to open, and when they are fully open, she thrusts out her hands to freeze Kiara.

"Take care of the rest of them!" I tell JJ.

I rush over to Zoë and pick her up. I carry her to the lawn of the next house, and Talia follows. She forms a forcefield around the three of us.

"Zo, are you okay?" I ask her anxiously.

She nods weakly.

"Do you know where Carter is?" I say.

She nods again and points at the sky.

"Huh?" I mutter, looking up at the sky.

"Zoë, I don't see anything," Talia says.

We keep looking.

"Oh my goodness," I gasp.

"What?" Talia demands.

"It's Carter."

Up in the sky is Carter. Flying.

Chapter 20

Carter starts to fly down, zooming towards us at an alarming speed.

"Break the forcefield," I order.

Talia looks confused.

"Just do it," I say.

She breaks the forcefield, just as Carter lands next to us. He picks up Zoë and then attempts to start flying again. It takes him a moment to get off the ground, and when he does he is a little wobbly.

"Get her somewhere safe," I tell him, and he nods.

"And since when can you fly?" I demand, trying to hide how impressed I am. He just discovered this power, and he's already flying all around.

"I'll tell you later," he laughs, and rises higher in the air, flying off with Zoë, unnoticed.

"Let's go help JJ," I say to Talia.

We run over to the lawn of Joy's house.

"What's going on?" I ask when I take in the scene.

JJ is standing there, by himself. Lizzie, Saria, Logan, and the rest of them are all lying, frozen, on the ground. Joy is ushering all of the non-attackers out of the house.

"You're not the only one who discovered a new power today, Alavis. I have ice powers, like Zoë. They were pretty easy to defeat since they only had daggers, which I froze. They'll probably unfreeze soon, though. It's pretty hot out," JJ explains excitedly.

"That's awesome, JJ!" I exclaim, my eyes drifting over to the front door of the house.

As the last people exit, Joy shuts the door.

"We should get out of here," I tell JJ, and he nods in response.

"Okay. Bye Joy! Thank you for letting us stay with you! We

have to go!" I shout quickly, and then we run off down the road.

"Where are Carter and Zoë?" JJ inquires as we run, the cozy houses a blur as we speed past them.

"Carter can now fly, and he took Zoë off somewhere safe," I reply.

Talia sighs frustratedly. "How are we going to find them?"

"And where are we going?" I add.

"Carter's smart. He'll find us. In the meantime, let's go back to our ship, and start looking for your sister," JJ says calmly.

"Okay. What planet are we going to first?" I ask.

"We'll figure it out on the ship."

"Sounds good. And I think I see Carter!" I exclaim, pointing to the sky.

Carter flies down, and lands next to us, his curly hair falling into his eyes. Zoë jumps out of his arms and hugs me.

"We're heading to the ship," I tell Carter.

"Cool. We should run though. We don't want them catching up with us," he replies.

We all start to run again but have to stop a minute later. My knees buckle, and I collapse onto the dirt road.

"The Fatiga is hitting me," I mumble.

Carter and Zoë have collapsed next to me, and JJ and Talia both look exhausted as well.

"I forgot about Fatiga," groans Talia.

"What's Fatiga?" asks Carter, his voice barely a whisper.

JJ explains quickly, "It's what you are feeling right now. Magic drains you. As you get stronger, the Fatiga will be less strong, or at least that's what our teacher said."

"We need to keep moving," I mutter.

"We'll just stay here a couple minutes longer," JJ says, lying down on the ground.

"Just a couple minutes," I repeat as I drift off to sleep.

* * *

"GET UP!" shouts a voice.

I am jolted awake, and I sit up quickly. As I start to get up off the ground, I notice that the Fatiga is mostly gone.

"It's been half an hour! We need to go!" Talia yells.

"I didn't go to sleep, despite my tiredness. I tried to wake you all, but I couldn't," she adds bitterly.

"Sorry, Talia," JJ says, standing up.

Carter stands as well.

"Let's go," I say.

Zoë, however, remains on the ground.

"Zoë, we have to go," I tell her gently.

"I know," she mumbles.

"You're going to ride on my back, ok?" I say.

She nods, and slowly stands up. She hops on my back, and we start walking.

"Are we close to the ship?" Talia asks tiredly.

JJ shrugs. "I don't think so, but I don't really know."

"Carter, can you go fly ahead and look?" I suggest.

"I just got my energy back, Alavis," he sighs.

"We'll get there eventually. It's fine," Talia says.

We walk for two hours until finally, the ship comes into view.

"Thank goodness," Zoë smiles, morphing into a dog.

She runs ahead of us, barking happily. Being with Zoë makes me miss Artemis even more. The whole two hour walk, all I could think about was Artemis.

"How will we find Artemis?" I ask my friends.

"I don't know, Alavis. We'll figure it out," Talia sighs, the annoyance in her tone clear.

"I'm sick of that! We need to figure it out now!" I cry, tears starting to roll down my cheeks.

"Stop crying. You're 14, Alavis," Talia snaps.

I glare at her.

"All right, everyone calm down. We don't need another big fight," Carter says quickly.

Frustratedly, I pick up my pace so that I'm walking ahead of all of them. About 25 minutes later, I'm at the ship. Everyone is still a little bit behind me, so I sit down cross-legged on the grassy field to wait for them. All of a sudden, the space in front of me fills with smoke. Coughing, I squint to see the figure appearing in this smoke. After a moment, the air is clear again, and a shadowy figure stands in front of me. I scream. Loudly. Immediately, flames flicker to life in my palms.

"Now, now, don't scream," the shadowy figure scolds.

The fire in my palms grows larger, and I glance behind me.

"Ah, your friends are here," the figure notices.

"Who is that?" Talia demands, coming up next to me. She forms a forcefield around all of us.

"A forcefield will not help you," sneers the figure.

"Who are you?" JJ yells.

The shadowy figure snaps its fingers to reveal a tall man

with short, neatly cut brown hair. He wears a plain black uniform with a small, gold "E.M." on it.

"I am the messenger of the Queen. She wishes to see you," the man announces, pointing at me.

"The Queen of what? And why does she want to see me?" I ask.

The man looks surprised. "The Queen of Elvaqua, of course."

Chapter 21

“**W**hy does the Queen of Elvaqua want to see me?!” I gasp. “I can’t tell you that information,” the man shrugs. He snaps his fingers, and the door to our ship opens up.

None of us move. We just stand there, staring at the open door.

“Please drop the forcefield,” says the man. I can tell by his tone that this is not a request. It’s a demand.

“No way,” Talia replies, her voice sharp like a blade.

“If you would just get rid of the forcefield, we can get on the ship and go,” the man explains in an annoyed voice.

"NO WAY!" Talia repeats, more forcefully this time.

The man's eyes narrow, and the grass outside of the forcefield starts to turn a deep gray color. The bright blue sky darkens.

"I have a piece of information that may persuade you," the man tells me.

"What?" I demand.

"We have your sister," he says slowly.

My heart skips a beat, and my hands start to shake.

"Y-you have her?" I whisper.

The man nods.

"Is she alive? Did you hurt her?!" I ask him, raising my voice.

The man replies with a satisfied grin, "She is alive. And no, we did not hurt her. Just drop the forcefield, and I will bring you to her."

"Talia, get rid of the forcefield," I order.

"Alavis, this is probably a trap. The Queen will take our magic, or kill us!" Talia exclaims in frustration.

"I don't care. I want to see my sister!" I say firmly.

"They might not even have her. He's lying, Alavis!" Talia cries, trying to convince me.

"Talia, we're not going to change her mind," Carter sighs.

"I know," Talia mutters bitterly.

"When you drop the forcefield, you guys run," I say quietly. "Turn invisible, fly, whatever. Just get out of here. I'm going to see my sister, but I won't put you all in danger."

"We're not leaving you," Zoë insists, jutting out her chin.

Talia looks like she wants to disagree, but then she nods. "Zoë's right. We're coming with you."

"I can't ask you guys to do that," I sigh.

What I don't say is that, if they get hurt, it will be all my fault. And I don't know if I could live with that guilt.

But looking around at their determined faces, I know that they are going to come. Even though I haven't known them all for very long, they're starting to feel like family to me.

"You're not asking. We're insisting," JJ says.

"We're coming, whether you like it or not," Carter adds resolutely.

"Are you sure?" I reply.

"No, not really," mutters Talia.

JJ gives her a look.

"I'm kidding. Let's go," she says.

The force field disappears, and we march onto the ship,

the door shutting behind us. I watch the messenger from Elvaqua closely as he sits down in one of the seats. I really hope I'm not making the wrong decision here. I sit down in a seat as well and buckle my seatbelt. What I'm doing may be dangerous, but I have to do it, for Artemis. I take a deep breath as I start to get excited. I'm going to see Artemis. I'm going to see Artemis!

It's a trap, A voice reminds me in the back of my mind. I push the thought away. I know that I could be walking into a trap, but I have to see Artemis.

"We will arrive in a couple weeks," the man informs us.

"Do you have a name?" JJ asks suddenly.

The man looks surprised. "I am usually just called Messenger. But my name is Alec," he tells us.

"Well Alec, I'm going to assume we are walking into a trap here, no?" JJ sighs.

"I cannot tell you that," Alec states.

"Yeah, yeah, I know," grumbles JJ.

* * *

I wake up in the middle of the night to hear voices arguing. We're back to all sharing a room since it's the same ship we came here on. I miss having my own room, like I did at Joy's house. At least Alec isn't in the room with us. He's sleeping in the living room. Speaking of which, how did Alec get here? I didn't see another ship, but he must have come on one. I sigh. I'm too tired to contemplate that, and I pull my pillow over my head to try to go back to sleep. Unfortunately, the voices get louder.

"She's out of her mind!" snaps one voice.

Sounds like Talia.

"She wants to see her sister!" replies another voice, JJ, I think.

"This is crazy! We're heading straight into a trap. Elvaqua is the worst planet, remember? They took the Masthinyans' magic, and they will take ours! Why did I say we should come with her?" Talia hisses.

JJ sighs in exasperation. "She's our friend. Besides, Talia, were you really going to let a 14-year-old who has never been trained in magic go to Elvaqua alone? She'd get herself killed, and she'll be too emotional about her sister to think straight!"

"We shouldn't have come!" Talia yells.

I hear a groan.

"I'm trying to sleep," moans Carter.

"Too bad," Talia responds.

She and JJ go back to arguing, and a minute later, Carter speaks again.

"Can you just shut up so I can sleep? Alavis wants to see her sister, so we're going, and that's that. You said that we weren't leaving her. You could have walked away, Talia, and you didn't, so stop complaining," he mutters.

There is a second of silence, and then a loud yelp. I jump off the bunk bed that I'm on.

"What is going on?!" I cry, turning on the lights. "Is someone hurt?"

"What's wrong with you, Talia?" scowls Carter angrily.

He is lying on the floor, blood running down his cheek.

"Are you okay?" I ask, rushing over to him.

JJ runs out of the room, and returns with a first aid kit. While Carter wipes away the blood, I scan the room for Talia. After a moment, I spot a panther, black like midnight, its yellow eyes staring at me creepily. It stands in the corner of the room, a menacing look on its face.

I march over. "What the hell is wrong with you?!"

The panther morphs into human form.

"He was being rude!" Talia snaps, her eyes stormy.

"You attacked your friend!" I respond.

"He'll be fine. It's a little cut," shrugs Talia, not looking apologetic.

"Apologize to him!" I order.

"No."

"Apologize!"

"NO," Talia yells, morphing into a small green bug.

She scurries off, and I lose sight of her.

"She needs to control her temper!" I grumble, sitting down on the edge of Zoë's bunk.

Zoë puts her head on my shoulder.

"Is Carter going to be ok?" she whispers.

Before I can answer, Carter plops down next to us.

"Don't worry, Zoë. I'm okay. I know there's a lot of blood, but really it's just a tiny little cut," he says to her, pointing at his cheek. "So don't worry about me, okay?"

"Okay. What's wrong with Talia?" Zoë asks.

"She ... uh ... Well, she has a difficult time controlling her temper," I explain quietly.

"I'll talk to her," JJ says with a sigh, leaving the room.

"Talia! Where are you?" I hear him shouting.

"Zoë, why don't you go back to sleep," I suggest.

I'm too angry and stressed to go back to sleep anytime soon, but Zoë should at least get some rest.

"No thanks," she replies stubbornly.

"Okay," I sigh, and turn to Carter. "What are we going to do?"

"I don't know. She has to learn that just because you're upset doesn't mean you can turn into a panther and scratch someone's face," Carter mutters.

I groan. "But how are we supposed to help her control her temper?"

"I don't know," he repeats.

Chapter 22

Three days later, I still haven't seen Talia. I also haven't seen Alec, for that matter.

"This is crazy! How is she eating? Where is she?" JJ says, stomping into the kitchen.

He's been a wreck since Talia disappeared. I watch as he opens cupboards and drawers and then slams them closed, searching for the tiny bug that Talia turned into.

"She's obviously still on the ship. She's probably just crawling around somewhere in bug form, sneaking into the kitchen when we're not there," I say reassuringly.

JJ glares at me.

"She's usually completely fine at controlling her temper. I think you're the problem, not her!" he scowls at me.

I stand up, fireballs immediately forming in my palms.

"Hey! This is not my fault!" I snap.

"It is! You're the one putting our lives in danger, so you can have a nice little reunion with your sister!" JJ yells.

The fires in my palms grow, and the room becomes smoky.

"I told you to run away! You didn't have to come!" I shout back furiously.

"That's enough, both of you!" Carter says loudly, coming into the kitchen. "Alavis, put the fire away."

I sigh, but ultimately I do as he says.

"Let's all sit down to breakfast. Can one of you wake Zoë?" Carter asks, starting to prepare the food.

"I will," I mumble.

But, right before I exit the kitchen, I use my newfound ability and send a gust of wind toward JJ. He is knocked backward into the cabinets.

"Hey! I will turn you into an ice statue!" he threatens.

"I don't think so," I reply, rushing out of the room.

The floor of the spaceship feels cool beneath my bare feet as I make my way to the bedroom. The metal door is locked. Why would it be locked if Zoë is just asleep in there? Usually, the first person awake unlocks it and then we leave it unlocked for the rest of the day. Panic builds in my chest, and I try to push it away. There is probably a reasonable explanation. I knock on the door. Maybe Zoë is actually awake already and just wanted some alone time.

"Who is it?" mumbles a voice.

That is not Zoë. But it is a voice I recognize.

"Talia, it's me. Alavis," I tell her.

"Oh."

"Um ... Is Zoë in there?" I ask, unsure what to do.

"Yeah. She's still asleep," Talia replies.

"How did you get in?"

"The bedroom door was unlocked," she says.

"Oh. Right."

"So..uh...do you want me to wake Zoë up or something? I'm guessing that's why you came to the room," Talia asks awkwardly.

"Can you just open the door?" I say.

"Right, yeah. Sorry," she replies quickly.

A moment later, the door swings open, making a loud groaning noise. Talia stands in the doorway, her sky blue eyes rimmed with red, her cheeks wet.

"Are you all right?" I ask cautiously.

"I'm fine," she mutters, rubbing her eyes.

I follow her into the room and see Zoë sleeping peacefully on one of the beds. I kneel down next to her.

"Hey, Zo? Time to get up," I say.

She mumbles something but keeps her eyes shut.

"Zoë, we're having breakfast. It's time to get up," I repeat.

She keeps her eyes closed, and I'm about to tell her to get up again when she disappears.

"Zoë?!" I cry.

"Is she using her invisibility?" Talia suggests.

"Maybe," I reply, my heart pounding.

I reach out to tap where Zoë's shoulder would be but feel nothing there.

"So she isn't invisible," says Talia, panic creeping into her voice.

"Run and get the others," I order frantically, turning away from the bed to face her.

"Okay," Talia responds.

Right before she leaves the room, I hear a rustle. I whirl around, and sitting on the bed is Zoë, along with JJ.

"Zoë!" I sigh with relief.

"What just happened?" JJ asks, a confused expression on his face.

"I-I don't know. I just was thinking about how I didn't want to get out of bed. I was imagining how nice it would be to just appear in the kitchen, so I wouldn't have to walk all the way there, and—" Zoë starts.

"The kitchen is a two-second walk," Talia interjects.

JJ's face lights up, now realizing that Talia is here.

"Talia!" he exclaims.

He runs over to her and gives her a kiss.

"Where have you been?!" JJ says.

"Let Zoë finish," I tell them, nodding at Zoë.

"I was tired, Talia. So I didn't want to walk all two seconds, ok? Anyway, all of a sudden, I just appeared in the kitchen. I bumped into JJ, and then we appeared back here," Zoë explains.

Talia, JJ, and I all exchange a look.

"Teleportation!" I say with excitement.

Chapter 23

It's been a week or two now since Zoë discovered her new power. She's been practicing it by teleporting around the ship, and she's gotten pretty good at it.

"We are almost there. Be there in a day probably," Alec announces.

This is the first time I've seen him in days.

Talia nudges me, and I sigh. She wants me to have a talk with Zoë before we arrive. I asked Talia why she couldn't do it, but Talia said I'm Zoë's favorite, so it has to be me. I bend down so that I'm at eye level with Zoë.

"Zoë, when we get there, some bad things might be waiting for us," I start.

Her eyes widen. "W-what kind of bad things?" she whispers.

I put my hand on her shoulder. "The Elvaquins stole Joy and her friends' magic, remember?"

Zoë nods.

"They might try to steal ours too," I tell her.

"Then why did we agree to go with Mr. Messenger?" says Zoë.

I glance up at Talia, who is giving me a look.

"Stop it, Talia," I hiss, and then turn back to Zoë. "Well, I have a little sister, and they have her there—"

"Oh, right. I remember now," Zoë nods.

"Right. So, we're going to get her, and then get out of there as fast as we can," I finish very quietly. Don't want Alec to hear anything.

"What if there are others?" Zoë inquires.

"Others?" I reply, confused.

"If they have your sister, what if they have others trapped there too?" she clarifies.

"I ... I never thought of that ... oh my goodness! I got it!" I exclaim.

"Got what?" asks Talia.

"That's where they were taken! When the people from the Marden were taken away, they must have been brought to Elvaqua! That's why my sister is there!" I explain.

"Yeah obviously. You didn't realize that before?" replies Talia.

I glare at her, feeling stupid.

"We have to free all of them too, then," Carter says, flopping down in one of the seats.

Talia sighs, "We'll discuss that later. Alavis, finish telling Zoe what she may need to do."

"Right. So Zoë, we're probably going to need your teleportation when we need to get out of there, okay? So you have to be ready," I say in a hushed voice.

I glance over to where Alec is sitting. It doesn't look like he heard anything.

"Yes. Can I try teleporting all of you now?" Zoë asks.

"Sure. Let's move to a different room first though. We don't want Alec seeing your power," I murmur.

We head into the kitchen, where JJ is eating lunch. Zoë takes my hand and Talia's.

"Talia, grab JJ's hand. Alavis, take Carter's hand," Zoë orders.

Suddenly, there are butterflies in my stomach, and my cheeks feel all hot.

"Alavis?" Zoë says, glancing at me.

"Sorry," I reply, taking Carter's hand. I take a deep breath to try and calm my nerves.

"Okay, here we go," announces Zoë.

She closes her eyes, and then suddenly, we're not in the kitchen anymore. We're in the bedroom. Then we're in the cockpit. Then back in the kitchen. I grab onto the counter to steady myself, my stomach feeling like I have just been dropped a couple hundred feet.

"That's awesome ... but I think I might throw up," I say to Zoë, forcing a smile.

"You'll be fine. That feeling should go away in a couple minutes," Zoë tells me. She looks like she's about to faint from exhaustion.

"Hey Zo, how about you go lay down?" I suggest.

"I'm okay," she replies, stumbling and nearly hitting her head on the table.

I sigh, "No, you're not. Go lay down."

Lifting her up, I carry her to the bedroom and set her down on one of the bunks. She immediately falls asleep, and I go back to the kitchen.

"One day till we get to Elvaqua. Why did I come along?" Talia is muttering.

"I didn't tell you to," I remind her.

"You basically did," Talia says.

"No, I didn't!"

"You think I was going to let an untrained 14-year-old go alone to Elvaqua?!"

"That's enough. Can't you two go five seconds without fighting?" Carter asks loudly.

"I could. It's Alavis who always picks fights with me!" Talia snaps.

"Excuse me?!" I reply.

"You are both impossible!" Carter cries, storming out of the room.

Chapter 24

"Welcome to Elvaqua," Alec says as we exit the ship.

"Thanks," JJ replies sarcastically.

I step onto the grass and am immediately hit by the smell of pine trees. Alec, ignoring JJ's sarcastic reply, leads us to the edge of a nearby river. I can't help but smile at the beautiful nature surrounding me.

Alec points to a sparkling, golden sailboat a few feet away from us. "That's our ride."

We step into the boat, and Alec pulls out a long, thin, silver stick.

"What is that?" I ask curiously.

"A wand, of course," he says.

"A wand?"

"Yes. We Elvaquins are witches and wizards. Did you not know that?" he asks.

"No. I'm afraid I wasn't taught that while I was locked up for five years," I scowl.

"Oh. Well then, off we go," he shrugs.

He points the wand at the sail, and we begin to move. As we go, I stare at the tall pine trees growing on both sides of the river. I've been out of the Marden for many weeks now, but I still get excited to see nature. I went five years without going outside, after all.

"This is the River Mailena. Named for our beloved Queen," Alec tells us.

"Does the name of the river change every time you get a new queen?" JJ asks.

"Yes."

"That's confusing."

"So?"

"Anyway," I interrupt. "I want to be taken to my sister first thing."

"You must see the Queen first," Alec says.

"No."

"You MUST see the Queen first," he repeats insistently.

"I will see my sister first," I snap.

"I really must follow my Queen's orders and—"

I form a fireball in my hand.

"I'm going to see my sister first," I growl.

Alec laughs. "Do not threaten me," he says, pointing his wand at the fire.

The flames extinguish, and my jaw drops open.

"You are not more powerful than us Elvaquins. See how easily we took the Masthinyans' magic?" Alec says.

I blow a gust of wind at him, and he falls off the boat. "Ha."

But sadly, a moment later he appears back on the boat.

"A wand is better than having just a few powers," he smiles.

I'm really starting to hate this guy.

* * *

A half an hour later, the Queen's castle comes into view. It's humongous, and it's made entirely out of gold and marble.

"It's beautiful," I murmur.

"I was expecting a dark and gloomy palace with gargoyles flying around," JJ says.

"Yeah, me too," Carter agrees.

Zoë whispers, "Alavis?"

"What's up?" I reply.

"I-I'm really scared," she tells me quietly.

I kneel down next to her. "I'm so sorry, Zoë. We should have left you with Joy."

"Then her friends would have attacked me," Zoë points out.

"I know, but I should have left you someplace safe," I insist.

"I wanted to help," she protests stubbornly.

"I know. But listen to me, ok? If things get bad, which I bet they will, teleport yourself out," I tell her.

"What about you guys?" she asks worriedly.

Talia comes over to us. "If we can all get out, that's great. But we want you to be safe," Talia explains.

"But—"

"Zoë, we're almost there. Remember what Talia and I just told you," I cut her off.

If anything happens to Zoë ... I take a deep breath. I won't let anything happen to her. Walking away, I stare off into the distance. Brightstar glitters overhead as we glide across the river. I glance at Alec, who has his wand clenched tightly in his hand. He points it at the sail, and we start to move extremely fast. Seeing this, an idea starts to form in my head. If my father was from Elvaqua, could I be ...

"We're here," Alec announces.

I'll have to figure that out later. Alec steps out of the boat, and we follow him. He gives a little flick of his wand, and the boat races back to the other side of the river.

"We will now see the Queen," says Alec, fixing me with a cold stare.

He waits a few moments, daring me to object, and then grins. Using his wand, he summons a sparkling gold carriage for us. With the amount of money I bet it took to make this luxurious carriage, Artemis and I could have had full stomachs for a month.

We climb in, and the carriage starts along the smooth gray road. Zoë holds onto my hand tightly, her face turning pale. I feel awful. She shouldn't have come. I should have... well I don't know. But I should have done something!

"It's ok, Zo. Don't worry," I whisper to her.

She puts her head in my lap, her whole body shaking.

"Do you want to teleport away? You can take Carter, and go back to the ship. He knows how to fly it. You can go to Camden, or one of the other planets," I suggest quietly.

She stares up at me, her emerald green eyes filled with determination. "No. I want to help you get your sister back."

"That's really sweet, Zoë. But you should get out of here. You should—"

"Alavis, I've got a lot of powers, and I'm strong. I can help! And if you try to force me to go back, I won't," Zoë says, straightening her shoulders.

I can still see fear in her eyes, and I so badly want her to go back, but I know that she won't leave.

"Okay. But promise me you'll be careful? And you'll teleport out if I tell you to?" I insist.

"I promise."

The carriage comes to a sudden stop, and I look up. We have halted in front of the entrance to the castle, the huge structure looming over me intimidatingly.

"We have arrived at the palace of our beloved Queen Mailena," announces Alec.

Chapter 25

Two guards stand at the main entrance of the palace, their eyes narrowed at us. Alec steps forward and holds out his wrist. The guards examine the golden bracelet he is wearing and then nod. The doors swing open, and before we go in, Alec hands one guard a handful of Silvers. The coins glitter in the sunlight, and Alec murmurs something to him about this being what he owes for his new wand. Then, we walk inside. The temperature in the palace is about 10 degrees cooler than the outside, and I find myself wishing I had a coat. We walk silently down the dimly lit corridors until we find ourselves in a large throne room. It takes my eyes a moment to adjust to the room's brightness. Upon the glittering golden throne sits the Queen. At least I assume it's the Queen. She has extremely pale skin, unnaturally blue eyes, and long white-ish blonde hair with a crown resting on top. She wears a black jumpsuit with a braided gold belt. I glance at the golden chaise in the corner of the room and the golden chandelier hanging from the ceiling. I'm noticing a bit of a color theme here. The Queen must really love gold.

"The Marden escapees and their little band of thugs. What a pleasure," snarls Queen Mailena.

Alec bows. "Your Majesty."

"Yes, yes. Good job bringing them. Now leave us, Messenger," she snaps.

Alec rushes off, and I almost feel bad for him, despite how rude he was to me earlier.

The Queen fixes her eyes on me. "Alavis Hansen. Lance's daughter. A nice boy. Your mother seemed all right, too." She pauses, sighing loudly. "It's a shame I had to kill them."

My heart skips a beat. "What did you just say?"

"You heard me. I killed them."

She killed my parents. She. Killed. My. Parents. The other

noises in the room are drowned out by the sound of my heart beating in my chest. My parents are dead because of her. My blood boiling, I take a step towards her. She smiles as if enjoying my pain. I scream, and the next thing I know, the entire room is on fire. The only area with no flames is the spot my friends are standing in. A laugh echoes through the room and Queen Mailena walks through the flames, her sparkling gold wand held out in front of her. I can see that she has created a forcefield to protect her from the fire. With a flick of her wrist, the raging fire is gone.

"Very good, child. I see you have fire powers, just like your mother. But I'm afraid you can't take me down that easily. Your parents would have been proud, though," she shrugs.

"Why did you kill them?" I demand, my voice breaking.

"When they realized our plans to attack Masthinya and take everyone's magic, they left. Didn't matter much to me, but then they decided to come back years later. I knew I smelled trouble, and so I flew to Masthinya. And when I arrived, they said they were here to help defend their planet. Abandoned their poor children because they cared more about Masthinya than you and your sister. Not great parenting if you ask me. They claimed they wanted a proper home for their kids, and they had to come back and help if it wasn't too late. So naturally, I had to kill them," explains the Queen.

"WHAT DO YOU MEAN, 'NATURALLY, I HAD TO KILL THEM'?" I shout.

"Well, Lance was a powerful wizard. I had heard that your mother was powerful as well. I couldn't have them helping out the Masthinyans when we were ready to take their magic. That would ruin our whole plan!" she says.

I clench my fists, ready to lunge at her when I feel a hand on my shoulder.

"Alavis, she'd kill you before you could even punch her," Carter whispers.

"She killed my parents," I reply.

"I know. But we have to focus on saving your sister right now," he says.

"She killed my parents," I repeat.

"Alavis. Focus on Artemis," Carter says.

I nod but don't unclench my fists.

"Now children, I'm afraid I'll have to kill you," says Queen Mailena with a mockingly sympathetic smile.

Chapter 26

"I was told I would get to see my sister," I snap, my heart racing. How did everything go wrong so quickly?

"That was a lie, my dear," the Queen shrugs in response.

She points her wand at me. Then suddenly, a teenage girl enters the room with a stack of books balanced on her head. In her hands, she has an open book, and she reads as she walks. Her hair is light blonde and is in a braid crown. Her eyes are the same unnatural blue that Queen Mailena's are, and she wears the same jumpsuit. The Queen sees her and her expression becomes annoyed.

"Enna. You are not supposed to be in here. Explain yourself," the Queen snaps, her wand still pointed at me.

Who is this girl?

"Enna!" the Queen shouts when the girl doesn't look up.

The girl, Enna, still does not respond. She merely continues to read. The Queen moves her wand away from me and points it at the book. It floats out of Enna's hands and over to the Queen. Enna is unfazed and takes a book off of her head. She starts to open it.

"Guards!" the Queen says with a frustrated sigh.

The guards in the room surround Enna and try to grab the books off of her head, but Enna quickly punches and elbows her way out.

"Really Mother?" Enna laughs.

This girl is the Queen's daughter?

"You are not allowed in this part of the castle, Enna," the Queen says.

She shrugs, suppressing a smile. "Oops. My mistake."

"Enna, do not be disrespectful to me," warns the Queen.

Enna ignores this comment and turns to us.

"Mother, who are these people?" she asks.

"Guests," Queen Mailena says nonchalantly.

I laugh, and the Queen narrows her eyes at me.

"Is something funny?" she demands.

"No. It's just...you called us guests," I say.

Enna looks at me with a confused expression.

"You are guests. Guests who I will soon kill, but guests nonetheless," the Queen shrugs.

Enna's jaw drops open in horror as she cries, "Mother!"

In my peripheral vision, I see Zoë trembling with fear, and I want to run over and comfort her. But I don't want to draw the Queen's attention to Zoë.

"What?" Queen Mailena replies to Enna, her tone annoyed.

"Y-you're going to kill them? You can't! They're only kids. What did they do to deserve this punishment?" Enna demands.

The Queen sighs in exasperation, pointing at Talia and me. "Those two escaped the Marden. They are too powerful, Enna. And these others working with them will only cause trouble. These children are a threat to Elvaqua."

"Wow. Five kids are a threat to your planet. I have to admit, I'm honored," smirks JJ.

Queen Mailena scowls.

"Mailena, I demand to see my sister!" I yell, tired of just

standing here waiting for Mailena to kill us.

"That is **QUEEN** Mailena, you disrespectful child!"

"You are not my Queen," I growl, my cheeks flushed with fury.

"Mother, you kidnapped her sister?!" Enna exclaims angrily.

"Enna, return to your room," orders Mailena.

Enna ignores her mother and instead marches over to my friends and me. She waves her wand at us, and we all disappear. We reappear in a small, dark storage room.

"What happened?" I ask confusedly.

"It's a simple bit of magic. Disappearing and reappearing somewhere else. Now, let's go find your sister," shrugs Enna.

"You're going against your mother?" I inquire.

"Yup. Always do. I despise her," Enna says.

I don't really trust this girl, but if she can help find Artemis ...

"I'm Zoë," Zoë introduces herself. "That's Alavis, Carter, JJ, and Talia."

"Zoë!" Talia groans. "Why did you tell her our names? You don't even know her."

"Nice to meet you," Enna responds, looking directly at Talia. Talia ignores her, saying, "We'll have to be invisible once we leave this room."

I watch as she purposely makes eye contact with everyone except Enna.

"If you keep ignoring me, I won't help you," Enna says.

I look at Talia pleadingly.

She sighs. "Fine. Hi Enna. Nice to meet you."

Enna smiles. "Now, what were you saying about invisibility?"

"We'll need to be invisible. JJ, I'll make you invisible. Zoë, just focus on turning yourself invisible. Alavis, you can turn Carter invisible?" Talia says, her eyes glinting mischievously.

"Sure," I reply, butterflies forming in my stomach.

"All right. I can get the guards to tell me where she's being held. Just stay invisible!" Enna says. "What's your sister's name?"

"Artemis Hansen."

Enna nods and then I take Carter's hand, and we turn invisible. Enna pushes the door open, and we head out into the hallway. We run into a guard almost immediately. He is throwing his weapon up in the air and catching it over and over again with a bored expression on his face. Enna smiles at him, and he comes to attention.

"Hello. I was curious where the prisoners were being held.

My mother ordered me to go check on a specific one. She worries that this prisoner may be plotting an escape. I was told to go and scare the prisoner so that she will no longer think about attempting to escape," explains Enna, her voice polite and formal.

"Princess Enna, I don't mean to be rude, but that sounds a bit suspicious," says the guard nervously, tugging at his beard.

Enna's eyes narrow. "You dare disobey the Princess? Or the Queen? These are Queen Mailena's orders!" snaps Enna.

The guard shuffles his feet. "I understand, Princess Enna. But you see, you have a bit of a reputation for making up stories and disobe—"

"Excuse me?" Enna snarls. She whips out her wand and presses it against the guard's throat. "Where is the prisoner, Artemis?" demands Enna. Her wand starts to glow a strange green color.

"Down this hall, to the right, down two flights of stairs. First cell on the left," the guard says quickly.

"Keys?" Enna asks.

He pulls a set of keys out of his pocket and drops them in Enna's hand. She returns her wand to her pocket.

"Thank you," she smiles.

Once we have turned right, and are out of earshot of the guard, Enna starts talking.

"I'll cover for you guys while you escape with Artemis. It'll be hard, but I know the castle well," she says.

"Enna, why are you helping us?" asks Talia skeptically.

"Why not?" Enna replies.

"Um, I don't know. Maybe because your mother is the Queen, and she wants to kill us," says Talia.

Enna crosses her arms over her chest. "I don't approve of how my mother leads. And I am my own person. I will not agree with something that is wrong just because my mother believes it is right."

We walk down the staircase and find ourselves in a damp, musty corridor. At first, the walls are just brick, but after we walk a bit more, we see the first cells. I turn to the first cell on the left. The door is made of some material that looks like glass, but I'm sure it is much stronger than glass. And lying in the corner, looking weak and frail, is my little sister.

Chapter 27

E nna hands me the set of keys, and I rush to the door. "Keep watch," I call over my shoulder. I insert one of the keys in the lock, but it doesn't work. I keep trying until I find the right key, and then finally, I hear a click. A keypad appears where the lock once was. "Guys? We need a code," I tell them.

Enna scowls frustratedly. "That guard didn't tell us that."

"How are we supposed to know what the code is?" cries Zoë, her eyes wide with concern.

Carter walks up to the keypad and studies it. He stands there studying it for about five minutes, and then he turns back to us. "5, 2, 7, 3," he announces.

"How did you figure that out?" JJ asks incredulously.

"I used my x-ray vision to look inside at the inner workings. Then by looking at that, I was able to figure out what buttons have to be pushed in order for the door to be opened," shrugs Carter casually.

"I forgot that you are a super-genius!" I exclaim excitedly, typing in the code. The door swings open.

"Artemis!" I cry, running to her side.

She opens her eyes a crack and smiles. Her face is pale, her dark blue hair knotted, and her hands are covered in a layer of dirt. There are bags under her eyes. "Alavis," she whispers.

"What happened to you?" I ask, tears forming in my eyes.

"T-they drained m-my magic. It nearly killed me. I'm not as strong as you are, Alavis," she replies.

Alec said they didn't hurt her, I think angrily.

"Yes, you are. You're the strongest person I know," I tell her, taking her hand in mine.

She laughs hoarsely. "I've missed you, Al."

"I've missed you too." I smile, hugging her. "Can you stand?

We're getting you out of here."

"I think so. Alavis, what about the rest? We have to free them too," Artemis says.

I nod. "I know." I toss the keys to JJ. "Go unlock the rest of the cells."

He gives me a thumbs-up and starts working on the next cell. Carter goes with him to figure out the code. While they do that, I help Artemis stand. She leans against me for support, and we walk out of the cell.

"Hi Artemis, I'm Zoë," Zoë introduces herself.

Artemis smiles. "Nice to meet you."

"That's Talia," I say pointing to Talia. "And Carter and JJ are over there unlocking the other cells, and that's Enna. She's the princess, but she's on our side," I say.

Artemis raises her eyebrows, looking skeptically at Enna.

"She helped us find you," I add.

"Okay," says Artemis, but she still looks suspicious.

I must admit, I'm still a bit suspicious of Enna as well. I sigh and glance over at JJ and Carter who are still working on opening the cells. I notice that the kids in the ones that have already been opened haven't moved.

"Guys, let's go help the kids. I think they are too weak from the magic draining to get up," I explain.

"Magic draining?" Talia cries in horror.

I nod grimly, and we each head into a cell. In the cell Artemis and I go into, there is a boy who looks to be a couple years older than me. He has shaggy auburn hair and hazel eyes. And he looks very familiar.

"Alavis, is that ... Darren?" Artemis asks me.

"I think so," I reply, shocked. "Darren?"

He glances at me and grins, his eyes brightening. "Hey, Al. Hey, Artemis. Long time no see."

I reach out my hand and help him up.

"Thanks. How've you been?" he asks, leaning against the wall for support.

"Not great. You?" I reply.

"Same. Artie, I didn't know you were stuck here too," he says, ruffling her hair.

"How do you guys know each other?" JJ asks curiously, helping a little boy out of one of the cells.

"Darren was Artemis' and my good friend back on the streets. He helped me take care of Artemis when she was little, and we worked together to get food and find places to sleep. Then, a few years before Artemis and I were taken to the Marden, he vanished. He was just gone. We assumed he had been taken to the Marden, and I guess we were right."

"The Marden really ruins everything," mutters JJ.

I nod in agreement before continuing. "Well, for many years, Darren was like a brother to me and Artemis, and we were so upset when he disappeared. But I knew that if I went looking for him, I would likely end up locked up in a cell. I'm sorry we didn't come looking for you, Darren," I say guiltily.

"Hey, don't be sorry. It wouldn't have done anything except gotten you thrown in the Marden. It was the smart choice," he shrugs nonchalantly.

"Well, we still ended up in the Marden. But yeah," I laugh, trying to ignore the gnawing feeling in my gut that Darren getting locked up is somehow my fault. I know that it wasn't. I just hate the idea that it happened, and I didn't do anything about it.

"Alavis, how are we going to get everyone out of the palace and to the ship without getting caught?" Talia interrupts.

"And speaking of getting caught, I may have threatened the guard into giving us the keys, but he's probably already called for backup. He was definitely suspicious of my reasons for wanting the keys," Enna adds.

"Good point. Let's get out of here," I say.

It takes us a little while longer to unlock all the cells, but eventually, everyone is freed.

"Can most of you walk?" I call out.

A lot of the prisoners nod.

"Okay, that's good. Help out the others who can't, okay?" I say.

They nod again, looking exhausted and downcast. As we walk through the prison hallway, I turn to Enna.

"Are there any guards in this place that seem like they want to rebel?" I inquire.

She looks at me, surprised.

"Maybe. There's one guard that always covers for me when I'm in trouble," she offers.

"That doesn't necessarily mean that this guard is a rebel," I sigh.

There has to be someone who can help us escape. We're going to need all the help we can get.

"The princess can help," suggests Enna.

I laugh. "Enna, aren't you the princess?"

"No, I mean my older sister. She can help us get the prisoners out," Enna explains.

"Oh, okay. But how is one extra person going to really help us?" I say.

"She's powerful. And she doesn't have a reputation like I do, so people in the palace will listen to her more. She could help create a distraction so you guys can get to wherever you need to go," says Enna.

"All right. Can you go get her?"

"Sure. But first, you all should hide until I get back," she tells me.

"Why? We're not weak, Enna. I can hold my own," I reply, a little upset at her lack of faith in my abilities.

"I'm sure you can. But some of these prisoners? Not so much," Enna says.

She pulls out her wand, and with a flick of her wrist, we all disappear. We reappear in a bedroom. The walls are light gray, and there is a canopy bed with seafoam green covers. The room is giant, which is good because there are hundreds and hundreds of prisoners.

Enna gestures around the room. "Just hang tight and stay put until I get back. Nobody will come looking for a bunch of prisoners in my room. This should only take a minute." Pushing open the door, she heads out.

I notice Zoë peering around the room. "Who are you looking for, Zo?"

"My parents. Maybe they're here." Her voice is filled with hope. She starts to make her way around the room, searching.

"So, Darren, no magic?" I ask, turning my attention to him.

"No magic," he agrees sadly.

"We'll get it back," I say.

His tone is disheartened as he replies, "That's optimistic thinking. Alavis, our magic is probably being stored somewhere in this palace. Once we escape, we're not coming back here to get it."

"Oh. I didn't think about that ... "

"If we want to get out of here safely, we have to leave our magic behind," says Darren dejectedly.

He's right. I have to get everyone out of here safely. That's more important than magic. However, if the Elvaquins have all this stolen magic, we're in serious danger, no matter where we go.

"You guys will go and get to safety. Enna and her sister must know where the magic is being stored, and I'll stay and try to find it.

If I don't, the Elvaquins will become too powerful. They'll try to take over. I know they will, and I can't let that happen," I decide.

Darren stares at me for a second and then laughs. "Yeah, right."

"What do you mean, 'yeah, right'? You don't think I can do it?" I snap, little flames dancing across my fingertips.

"No, no, you definitely could. Jeez, Alavis, put the fire away. I just meant that we're not just going to leave you here alone," he says.

"I'm not alone. I have Enna and her sister. I'll be fine," I remind him.

Darren shrugs. "I have no doubt that you will be, but we're still not leaving you behind."

"It's not leaving me behind! It's my choice, and I'll join you guys once I have your magic!" I cry in frustration.

"Fine! Go tell your friends your plan. See what they say," he responds.

I cross my arms over my chest angrily and sit down on the bed.

"Okay, I'll tell them," Darren says, marching over to everyone else.

I face the wall, which is covered in colorful paintings, as Darren tells them what I told him.

"Alavis, are you serious?" snaps Talia.

"I'm not leaving you. No way," Artemis adds, locking eyes with me. "I'm not going to lose you again."

"If you're staying, then I'm staying," Carter says.

Zoë returns from her walk around the room and sits down next to me.

"Were they here?" I whisper.

She shakes her head. "It's fine. I'm fine. And Alavis, we'll all stay and get back the magic with you."

"It's too dangerous," I sigh.

Carter groans.

"What?" I demand.

"You don't think we know that? I would like to point out that we are not completely useless. We can help," he says in exasperation.

"Um, I don't mean to be rude or anything, but why the hell are we staying here instead of trying to escape?" asks one of the freed prisoners.

She is tall, with wavy chestnut brown hair and bangs, and freckles splattered across her nose. Her gold-rimmed glasses start to slip down her face, and she pushes them back up in annoyance.

"I'm Olive, by the way," she adds.

"Alavis. Nice to meet you," I reply.

"So, about my question ... "

"I'll answer," says JJ. "Basically, you don't have magic, correct?"

"Correct," Olive replies sadly.

"Well, if the Queen has everyone's magic in her possession or something like that ... I don't really know how someone would go about storing magic ... but anyway, even if we escape, we aren't safe. With all that power, plus the power the Queen will gain once she drains the magic of every single person in all three Mardens, she will come for us. She will eliminate anyone who is a threat to her power. We need to stop her now before she can get any stronger," JJ explains.

"Makes sense," Olive shrugs. "And I do miss my magic."

I get up from the bed and glance around the room. "First thing first, does anyone here not want to stay and help? Don't be embarrassed, because it is totally fine. We can send you with ... " I pause to think. " ... Enna's sister, and she'll hopefully help get you out."

The room is silent, and then a few people raise their hands, mostly the younger ones of the group. I notice that Zoë and Artemis' hands remain by their sides.

"Artemis, Zoë, please go with them," I beg.

Zoë gives me a defiant glare, and Artemis' dark gray eyes narrow.

"Nope," Artemis says.

"No," Zoë agrees.

"Please ... I need to know that you guys will be safe. I can't put you in this kind of danger. Look, a lot of the other kids your age are going to leave. Go with them, please," I say.

"NO," Zoë shouts, the air turning cold.

The ground under my feet becomes slippery and icy.

"Zoë, stop it!" I snap.

"I'm staying!" she insists, everything in the room starting to freeze over.

"Zoë!"

"I'm staying!" she repeats.

"Fine, you're staying!" I sigh, relenting. "Now get rid of the ice."

She smiles and the temperature goes back to normal. The ice on the ground disappears.

I sigh again and turn to Artemis.

"Please?" I plead.

She shakes her head.

"Then you're going to have to learn to be a witch."

Chapter 28

Luckily for us, there is an extra wand sitting on the dresser. I guess it's there in case Enna loses hers, and I pick it up.

"I'm not Elvaquin. I'm not a witch," Artemis reminds me, pushing her knotty hair out of her eyes.

"Yes, you are. Dad was Elvaquin," I tell her.

She gasps. "He was?"

I can tell that she is excited to know something, anything, about our father.

"Yup. We're going to ask Enna to teach you a little self

defense," I explain.

"Did someone say my name?" asks a voice.

Enna appears out of thin air, a much older girl standing beside her. This girl looks nothing like Enna and the Queen; she has a very narrow face, curly, midnight black hair, and dark green eyes.

"This is the other princess, Catalina," Enna announces.

Catalina waves.

"Okay, let's ask the big question again," Talia sighs. "Why are you helping us?"

"Like Enna, I ... the Queen and I do not always see eye to eye," says Catalina carefully.

"Why?" asks Zoë.

Catalina swallows hard, trying not to cry. "I'm not technically the Queen's daughter. You see, I married her son, Prince Edward. And we were very happy together. But we decided we didn't want to stay here. Queen Mailena was too cruel. I told Edward that if we were ever to have children, we would not raise them here. I wouldn't allow it. So, we tried to leave. But Queen Mailena caught us. She tried to kill me and—" She pauses for a moment to compose herself, sitting down on the bed. "Edward stepped in front of me, and the spell hit him instead. Queen Mailena ended up killing her own son,"

Catalina manages to choke out.

"I'm so sorry," I tell her.

She nods, her eyes rimmed with red. "Queen Mailena won't let me leave. I've tried, believe me. But maybe with all of you with me, we'll be able to do it. And even if I can't get out of here, and live my life, I want to do anything I can to help you guys have a chance to go out and live your lives, free of Queen Mailena," she says, a determined look on her face. "I don't want her ruining any more lives."

"Actually, there's been a bit of a change of plans," I say, pointing to the group that is leaving. "Only some of us are going. Our spaceship is on the other end of the River Mailena. Get them on, and then all of you, get out of here. The rest of us need to find the stolen magic. After we find it, we need to steal one of the Elvaquin ships and leave."

"Oh. Okay," Catalina replies looking dejected.

I realize that I am sending her with a bunch of people who don't have magic, and are weakened from the draining. Why should her odds be any better this time? Maybe …

"Do you know how to fly a ship?" Talia asks her, snapping me out of my thoughts.

The Prisoner of Cell 47

Catalina smiles. "As a matter of fact, I do. Edward taught me," she says, her eyes tearing up again.

I hesitate. I know Catalina seems nice, but do I really want to send our newly freed prisoners, who don't have magic to defend themselves, with her? What if she turns out to be a psychopath like Mailena?

"What's wrong?" asks Carter, seeing the worried look on my face.

"I ... well ... " I stutter, unsure how to say this in front of Catalina.

Thankfully, Carter seems to realize what I'm thinking.

"Ah, I see. Well, one of us could go, too," he suggests.

"I suppose. But who?" I sigh.

This could solve both problems. In addition to the little possible psychopath problem, it also means that Catalina might have slightly better odds.

"I ... I'll go," Talia offers.

JJ looks at her in horror.

"Well, who else do you want to go?" she whispers.

He responds quietly, but I have very good ears.

"Me. I'll go with you," he says.

193

"We need our people with magic to stay here. This will be the harder job. Only one of us should go!" Talia replies.

"Well what about—"

"What about who? This was Alavis' idea, and she was planning on doing it alone originally. She'll want to stay. We'll need Carter's smarts to get back the magic more than we will to escape. And we are not sending a six-year-old alone with a bunch of people she doesn't know!" Talia whisper-shouts.

"No! Talia, I'm not leaving you!" JJ frowns.

"JJ! We have to! I'll see you soon, okay?" she says.

He looks at her pleadingly. "Please, Talia. Please don't go."

"JJ, I—"

"What if something happens? What if we never see each o—"

"JJ, don't. We're going to see each other again."

He nods shakily, and they both look at each other for another long moment.

JJ kisses her. "I love you, Talia."

"I love you, too. Goodbye," she whispers.

Talia walks over to Catalina, who is still sitting on the bed.

"Ready?" Catalina asks, and Talia nods.

The group that is leaving holds hands, and they disappear.

"I hope they don't run into too much trouble," says Darren.

I nod in agreement. Then, I glance over at JJ, who is trying very hard to hold back his tears.

"Let's go get our magic," I say.

Chapter 29

"It's a staff," Enna explains, sitting down cross-legged on the gray ottoman at the edge of her bed.

I lean against the dresser. "Huh?"

"That's where the magic is being kept. It's this special staff that holds the magic inside of it. I've seen Mom use it," Enna says.

"Like use it to give herself magic?" Darren clarifies, distractedly picking up a watch from Enna's nightstand.

Enna nods, and then adds, "Put that down."

I turn to my left to see how JJ is doing. His eyes are red, and he hasn't said a word since Talia left.

I tap him on the shoulder, and whisper, "Hey, are you okay?"

"Alavis?" snaps Enna.

I turn back towards her. "Yeah?"

"Am I boring you? This is your life on the line here!" she hisses, a murderous expression on her face.

I looked away for a second! Why is she so mad?! "I know that!" I reply, my hands starting to feel warm.

Carter gives me a look as he comes to stand next to me.

"What?" I demand.

He points at my hands, and I notice that there are tiny flames dancing across my palms, dangerously close to the wood of the dresser.

"Oops."

The flames disappear. Sometimes they just form when I'm upset. I can't help it!

"Alavis, you've got anger issues," mutters Enna.

"Thanks. I really appreciate that," I scowl.

Enna whips out her wand and points it at me, her blue eyes icy cold. "I don't appreciate your sarcasm," she growls.

"Woah, chill out, guys!" Olive says, glancing at us nervously.

"I didn't mean to form fire!" I say. "Why are you making such a big deal out of this?"

Enna stares at me for a moment longer and then looks away. "I'd watch your back if I were you, Alavis. With that personality, you're bound to have *many* enemies," Enna says, her voice full of malice.

"Shut up, Enna," mutters Carter.

Enna gets up off the ottoman, moving quickly over to Carter. She presses her wand up against his throat. "What did you just say?" demands Enna, her eyes blazing.

This girl takes everything way too seriously!

"I told you to shut up. I personally am beginning to wonder if you're really on our side," Carter replies calmly, pushing her wand away from his throat.

"Are you on our side?" he asks.

Enna pauses, glances at all of us, and then sighs. "Yes. I am."

"Okay. So how do we find the staff and get the stolen magic back?" Carter inquires.

Enna sits back down on the ottoman, explaining where the staff is located, but I'm only half listening. My heart is still pounding, and my brain is still screaming DANGER! The way Enna turned so quickly from the rebellious daughter into a mini-Mailena terrifies me. I push the thoughts out of my mind. I can't worry about that because whether we can trust Enna or not, right now she's our only shot at succeeding.

"Hey. You okay?" Carter whispers.

"What? Oh, yeah, I'm fine," I reply, forcing a smile.

"Maybe pay a little closer attention to what Enna is saying, though, or else she might try to attack you again," suggests Carter.

"Eh, I could beat her easily," I say jokingly.

"I'd be more scared for her than for you," Carter says, his expression completely serious.

"I was kidding. I'm sure she's way better at magic than me," I respond quickly.

"I doubt it. She's definitely not as nice as you are, that's for sure," shrugs Carter.

My cheeks turn red. "Uh ... thanks ... yeah ... um ... thanks ..." I stutter, and then quickly look away so he doesn't see me blushing.

"Alavis!" snaps Enna.

"Shush, Enna. She's having a moment!" Olive says, flopping down on the bed, grinning.

My face turns even redder, as Enna says to Olive, "Get off

my bed."

Olive ignores her, and Enna exasperatedly turns her attention back toward me.

"What is it, Enna?" I ask.

"Why can't you just pay attention?" Enna exclaims frustratedly.

"I'm sorry! Can you repeat what you were saying please?" I respond, trying to be polite.

"No. Ask your boyfriend. Maybe he was paying attention," grumbles Enna.

"He's not my boyfriend," I tell her quickly.

Enna laughs. "Yeah, sure. Okay."

I glance at Carter. His cheeks are just as red as mine, and he runs his fingers through his curly hair nervously.

Artemis, who is sitting on the floor in front of me, whispers, "Alavis, all Enna said was that the staff is in a secure vault in the basement of the palace."

"Thanks, sis," I reply gratefully.

"How do we break into this vault?" asks a guy, who I would guess is somewhere around 17 or 18. He has shaggy blonde hair, hazel eyes, and an impish grin. He also is very thin and frail, as are many of the prisoners in the room.

"I haven't exactly figured that out yet," sighs Enna.

"We need a diversion. Something big enough to get whoever's guarding the vault to leave," Carter suggests.

"Definitely," Enna nods. "The problem is, once we get the guards away, the staff is still heavily protected."

"What kind of protection?" inquires Carter.

"I have no clue. My mom doesn't tell me much," shrugs Enna.

"So we've got to be prepared for anything. What kind of diversion are we thinking?" I say.

The blonde guy raises his hand.

"You don't have to raise your hand," Enna mutters.

He puts his hand down sheepishly. "Hi. I'm August. I think that our best bet would be to all pretend to go after the staff. That's our diversion. We'll be stopped almost immediately, and there are so many of us, that they'll need all the guards to come fight. Nobody will notice if a little group is gone, and that little group can slip out of Enna's room while the fight's already happening. Then, they get the staff, and we all get out of here."

"That's actually a really good idea," Darren says.

"What do you mean *actually*? Why do you sound so

surprised?" August replies.

"It's just, back when we were cell neighbors, the escape plans you came up with were always... not so great," shrugs Darren.

"Excuse me?" August gasps.

"Hey, I'm just tellin' the truth, Auggie," Darren says.

August glares at him.

"Are you two done?" says Enna.

August nods but continues to glare at Darren. Enna starts to say something else but is interrupted by Carter.

"Sorry, Enna. But while that is a good idea, what happens once we have the magic, and once we give it back to everyone? What's stopping the Elvaquins from taking our magic again?" he asks.

"Let's take their magic," a girl with short, neon green hair calls out.

"That makes us just as bad as them," I remind her.

She mutters something about blue-haired, goody two shoes. Rude.

"Look, I know we have to figure this out, but we are really, really short on time. The guards are going to be searching for you guys. We need to move. Now," Enna says.

Artemis stands up. "I know we're short on time, but can you

teach me a little self-defense? Even just one spell," she asks, holding up the wand from Enna's dresser.

"You stole my w— Oh never mind," Enna mutters. She comes over to Artemis, pulling out an ivory wand, and she holds it in front of her. "I'm going to teach you two very important spells, and then we need to go," says Enna.

She glances nervously at the door, probably calculating how long we have until the guards burst through this door.

"Is there a wand for Alavis?" demands Artemis.

Enna sighs but grabs a silver wand from her desk drawer and hands it to me.

"Wait a minute. How do you expect to do Elvaquin magic? You're not Elvaquin," says Enna suddenly.

"My dad was," Artemis explains.

"Oh, okay. Well, didn't your magic get drained?" Enna asks, clearly confused.

"I'm hoping that was only my powers and not the Elvaquin magic," Artemis replies.

"We'll have to see. Just try it, I guess. Ok, so if you want to create a spell forcefield, whisper Protect. Focus all of your energy into the wand, and picture a shield surrounding you, deflecting any magic that comes your way," instructs Enna.

I close my eyes and whisper the word. When I open my eyes, I see... nothing.

"C'mon, Alavis, put all of your energy into it," Artemis tells me, surrounded by a shimmering golden bubble.

I guess the Elvaquin magic inside of her didn't get drained after all. I shut my eyes again. "*Protect*," I whisper. I tell myself to concentrate, but all I can think of is that if I don't get this, I'm going to look really bad in front of Carter...I mean in front of *everyone*. I don't care what Carter thinks.

Alavis, focus! I snap at myself.

I take a deep breath, imagining all of my energy flowing through the wand and into a shield. "*Protect*," I whisper.

"You did it!" exclaims Artemis excitedly.

I open my eyes and see that I am now also surrounded by a gold bubble.

"What exactly does this do though?" I ask.

"It's like a forcefield. It will deflect any magic thrown at you. It takes extreme focus though to maintain it, and extreme focus is not typically easy in battle," Enna explains.

"That's an awesome spell," Darren comments, grinning.

"Indeed," August agrees.

"All right, that was a very important protection spell. I'm now going to teach you one more spell, and then we will commence with the plan," Enna says.

"Not even a fully formed plan," JJ mumbles.

"Oh shut up," the neon green-haired girl says.

JJ gives her a look.

"Next spell. This will paralyze someone, which can give you a moment to catch your breath or whatever," Enna tells us. "Hold out your wand, and whisper *paralyze*. Pretty simple, no?"

My blood turns to ice at the word 'paralyze.' Memories of the Marden flood through me. Suddenly, I feel like I'm nine years old again, sitting alone in the cold cell. I remember my whole body trembling that first day, my throat raw from screaming. I remember the guard coming into my cell.

"Welcome to the Marden, kid," he had said, holding up the zapper. "This'll paralyze you if you misbehave. It's not a good feeling, let me tell you. I'd advise you to not cause any mischief."

"Alavis?" a voice says, jolting me out of my thoughts.

My sister's gray eyes are full of concern. "Are you all right?" she asks worriedly.

"I'm fine," I reply, shoving those Marden memories into the deep depths of my mind.

"Ready to try the spell?" Artemis smiles, and I nod.

"Who am I supposed to paralyze?" I ask.

"Oh. That's problematic," Enna sighs. "You'll have to try that one when you need it."

"Great," I mutter.

"Well, thank you Enna," says Artemis.

She puts her wand in her pocket, and I do the same. Suddenly, I hear loud footsteps in the hallway.

"I'll be right back," says Enna anxiously, going to check who is outside.

After five tense minutes of waiting, she comes back.

"Who was it?" I ask.

"Just some guards. I lied and told them Mother wanted them to check on some commotion happening in the dining hall. That's on the other side of the palace. Should keep them distracted for a little bit. That is, until they discover that there is actually no commotion," Enna says, looking a little shaken.

"Good thinking," Artemis nods.

Enna gives Artemis a quick smile and then opens a closet in

her room. It is full of swords, daggers, bows and arrows, and wands.

"If anyone else is part Elvaquin, grab a wand. Otherwise, take whatever you think you'll be best with. Now, who is going to get the staff? I think it should be the most powerful because it'll probably be very difficult to get to it. Mother won't have made it easy," Enna suggests.

"So Alavis should go," JJ says.

I give JJ a nod of thanks. I didn't want to sound like I was being arrogant and calling myself the most powerful or anything. I just want to go after the staff.

"I'll go too," Carter says immediately.

"I'll stay and fight," says JJ.

I glance at him, confused. Why doesn't he want to come with us?

"I'm going wherever Alavis goes," Artemis announces.

"Alavis?" Zoë whispers.

"What's up, Zo?" I reply.

"I'm kinda scared to fight. Can I go with you?"

"Of course," I say kindly.

"Right now, it's me, Alavis, Artemis, and Zoë," Carter states.

"Maybe one or two more," says Enna. "The defenses will be

difficult to get past."

"I'll go," a tall, muscular woman says. She looks like she is in her 30s or 40s, and has curly brown hair, dark skin, and dark brown eyes.

"I'm Gia," she introduces herself. "I was thrown into the Marden two years ago."

JJ gasps. "Gia? Is that really you?" he says, walking over to her.

Gia smiles. "Hello, JJ. I didn't see you in here before."

"I can't believe it's really you!" JJ exclaims, shocked.

"JJ, how do you know Gia?" I ask curiously.

"This is Talia's and my teacher," JJ explains. "She's as wise and strong as they come."

Gia glances around the room. "Talia's left, hasn't she?"

JJ's smile vanishes. "Yes. Sh-she's helping get some of those who don't want to fight to safety," says JJ, holding back tears.

"I see," Gia replies.

There is an awkward silence.

"Um, can I come, too? Not to sound selfish, but I want my magic back. Not that I don't trust you guys, but I want to be there so I can make sure I get it back," Olive says, breaking the quiet.

"Sure, Olive," I tell her.

"Can I come as well?" asks August, and I nod.

"I'll come, too," Darren adds.

"Ok, I think that's a good amount of people. Now, all of you, wait a couple minutes and then slip out that side door there. The basement staircase is at the end of the hall. Good luck," Enna says.

I run over to JJ and give him a hug. Carter and Zoë do the same.

"You sure you don't want to come with us to get the staff?" I ask.

"No. I want to fight. I'll see you all soon," JJ replies.

ChaptER 30

You know how sometimes three minutes can feel like three seconds and other times it feels like three hours? Well right now, three minutes is feeling like three weeks.

"How long has it been?" I ask anxiously.

Carter glances at the clock on the dresser. "It's only been a minute, Alavis."

"You're kidding," I sigh.

He shakes his head.

"Alavis?" Zoë says, fixing her bright green eyes on me.

The Prisoner of Cell 47

"Yes?"

"A-are people going to die?" she asks, her voice trembling.

"They might, Zo. They might," I whisper, trying not to show Zoë how scared I am.

"Am I going to die?" Zoë mumbles.

"No," I say immediately.

"How do you know?" she inquires.

"I won't let it happen. Zoë, I will not let anything happen to you, I promise, okay?" I tell her, fear gnawing at my heart.

Of course, I'll do everything I can to protect Zoë. But what if it's not enough? I did everything I could to protect Artemis and we still ended up in the Marden. It terrifies me that whatever I do might not be enough to save the people I love. I take a deep breath, pushing these thoughts away. Then, I clear my throat, and everyone looks at me expectantly.

"Listen, everyone. Though most of the guards are probably going to go fight, there will likely be some guards that stay at their posts. And, it's possible that the guards protecting the staff will stay there. We need to be ready. If you haven't already, you should grab a weapon," I say, pointing at the weapon closet.

Darren, August, Gia, and Olive head to the closet.

211

"Artemis, grab something, too," I advise.

"I have a wand," she reminds me.

"Yes. But you only know two spells."

Artemis walks over to the closet and takes a sword. Carter takes a sword as well, and I take a dagger, just in case.

"Zoë, you should take a weapon, too," I say.

She pulls a dagger out of her boot. "I already have one."

I recognize it as the dagger she had when we first met her on the spaceship.

"Okay, good." I check the clock again. "We leave in one minute," I announce.

Carter squeezes my hand. "You nervous?" he asks.

"Yeah. And we're not even going to be in the big fight," I reply, ignoring the butterflies fluttering around in my stomach.

"We have to get the staff quickly. The longer they have to fight ... " he trails off.

"The more people that ... " I swallow hard, struggling to say it. "The more people that die."

He nods, the gravity of the situation settling over the room like a storm cloud.

"What if we fail?" I ask quietly.

"We won't," Darren answers, coming over to me.

"This was so unnecessary. We should have just escaped. Who cares about our magic? Why did I even suggest it?" I sigh, burying my face in my hands.

"You were right to. Someone has to stop Mailena's plan," Carter assures me.

"But it doesn't have to be us. I never meant to put this many people in danger. I was just going to do it myself," I mutter.

"Everyone would be in danger even if we didn't try to get our magic back. We have to go now," Carter says, a hint of annoyance in his voice as he checks the clock.

I take a deep breath. "Okay, let's go. We should be invisible before we leave. Zoë, can you turn Olive, Gia, and August invisible? I'll turn Carter, Artemis, and Darren invisible," I say.

Zoë nods, and Olive and August hold her hands. Gia puts her hand on Zoë's shoulder. It takes half a minute, but eventually, they are all invisible. Darren, Carter, and I hold hands, and Artemis puts her hand on my shoulder. I close my eyes and concentrate. Approximately 15 seconds later, we are all invisible. Darren pushes open the side door with his free hand, and we tiptoe out into the hall. Almost instantly, I hear the clang of swords in the distance.

"Quickly," I whisper.

We make our way down the empty hall. Suddenly, a guard appears out of nowhere.

She can't see us, I tell myself, my heart pounding.

The guard holds up a locator, like the ones from the Marden. I guess that makes sense because it seems like the Elvaquins work with the Marden, or maybe even own the Marden. The air around us shimmers.

"Aha!" The guard smiles, pulls out a wand, and starts to whisper something.

"Artemis. Protect spell," I hiss.

Artemis whips out her wand and closes her eyes.

"*Protect,*" she murmurs.

A flickering golden bubble slowly forms around the four of us and then spreads to cover Zoë and her invisible gang, too.

"Stay focused, Artemis," I remind her.

She doesn't respond. I watch as the guard looks at her wand in shock.

"I don't hear any cries of pain. Spell must not have worked," the guard mutters frustratedly.

Suddenly, our protective bubble breaks.

"Artemis? What are you doing?" I snap.

She ignores me and whispers the word, *paralyze.* The guard yelps, and topples over, her limbs frozen.

"Great job, Artemis," I grin.

"I do know what I'm doing," she mutters, rolling her eyes at me.

We start to move down the hall again.

"I can hear you! I know you're there," the guard snaps.

"Should we run?" whispers Darren.

"I can't run and keep everyone invisible at the same time. I don't have the strength for that," I sigh.

"So let's just turn visible. The guard already knows where we are because of that locator thing," August suggests.

The air around us continues to shimmer.

"Okay," I reply.

I feel a weight lifted off my shoulders as we all turn visible, and I take a deep breath. Zoë and her gang turn visible as well.

"The guard probably won't be paralyzed for much longer," notes Artemis.

I try to take a step forward and collapse. I guess turning four people invisible can be a bit tiring. Carter catches me before I hit the floor.

His chestnut brown eyes are filled with concern. "Alavis, are you okay?"

"I'll be fine. Let's run. The guard won't be paralyzed for much longer, I'll bet," I reply.

He sighs. "Can you even run?"

"I have to," I snap.

"You kids spent too long talking," hisses the guard, getting up. She points her wand at Artemis, scowling furiously. "You paralyzed me."

She starts to murmur a spell. My friends seem to be frozen in place. I watch as Artemis fumbles with her wand, but she can't seem to get a protection spell working. Without hesitation, I jump in front of my little sister. A wave of pain rolls over my body as the spell hits me, and I crumple to the floor.

"NOOOO!" screams Artemis, kneeling down next to me.

I hear the sounds of fighting.

"They're taking care of the guard. Don't worry," Artemis tells me, tears in her eyes.

"Good," I say, managing a smile despite the fact that I feel like I am in a pool of fire, being stabbed over and over again.

"You can't die, Al. You can't," says Artemis.

"We don't know if the spell was meant to kill. I may just die from the pain, though," I murmur.

"Alavis!" cries Artemis, her voice shaking.

"Sorry," I say weakly.

"Stay with me, Al. Please," Artemis sobs.

"It's okay, Artemis. I love you," I whisper.

She clutches my hand, and the world goes black.

Chapter 31

I regain consciousness.

"She's alive!" shrieks a voice.

A blurry face swims in front of me. I blink my eyes a couple times and see that it is Artemis. Her face is wet with tears. I glance around and see that I am in some sort of dimly lit storage closet. Artemis helps prop me up against a wall, and then sits down next to me.

"How are you feeling?" she asks. The relief that I am alive is clear on her face.

"Fine, I guess," I shrug, not wanting to worry her.

I am still in a lot of pain, but it is bearable now.

"We need to go. The longer we take to get the staff, the longer the others have to fight," I say.

With Artemis' help, I stand up, and then she wraps me in a tight hug. Zoë comes over and hugs me next.

"Thank goodness you're alive," Zoë whispers.

"Alavis, you can't just almost die on us like that," scolds Darren.

"Yeah. That was a little rude," says August.

I roll my eyes.

"We need to get the staff," Olive reminds us. "Oh, and I'm glad you're okay, Alavis."

"Thanks," I say, smiling weakly.

"Are you all right to keep going?" Gia asks, a look of concern on her face.

"No. But it doesn't really matter," I sigh.

"Sadly, you are right. We're being counted on," says Gia.

Suddenly, Carter appears, and tackles me in a hug.

"You can't just do that!" he snaps.

"Do what?" I ask.

"I thought you were going to die!" he cries.

"Sorry."

"Guys, we need to go. Let's get that staff," Olive interrupts.

"Wait. How did we even get here?" I ask.

"We all fought the guard. It was like six on one, and then we dragged you down the hallway till we found a good place to hide," Darren explains.

"The staircase is basically right across the hall from this door," Artemis tells me. She pushes open the door and peers down the hallway. "All clear. But I can hear guards coming. The guard we fought must have called for reinforcements."

I stumble forward, leaning against the wall for support.

"I can carry you, Alavis," Gia offers.

"I don't want to make you do that," I reply.

"Don't worry about me," says Gia.

She throws me over her shoulder in a fireman's carry, and we all rush out of the closet, and to the stairwell. Down one flight, then another, then a third, until I lose count of how many flights of stairs we have gone down. But eventually, we reach a cold, dank basement. Gia puts me down, and Zoë immediately grabs my hand.

"Alavis, I'm scared," she whispers.

"You're going to be okay, Zoë. You just need t—"

"Suck it up, kid. I don't mean to be rude, but we've got important things to do. Stop whining," snaps Olive.

"Olive!" I exclaim in horror.

"Hey, it's the truth," she shrugs.

Zoë takes a deep breath, and lets go of my hand. "She's right. I-I'll be strong, Alavis. I promise," Zoë says, squaring her shoulders.

"I know you will, Zo," I reply.

"So, shall we go?" asks August, staring down the dark hallway ahead. "I'm assuming this is the way to the staff."

"Yep, let's go," says Olive impatiently.

I form a ball of fire in my hand to give us some light, and we start to walk. The hallway gets narrower as we get farther, and we are forced into a single file line. Suddenly, I hear a piercing shriek up ahead.

"Is everyone okay?!" I shout.

The only response is another scream. My heart is pounding. What's going on? The hallway begins to widen again, and I gasp. About five feet in front of me is Olive, her eyes lifeless, her body limp.

ChaptER 32

"The guard just appeared out of nowhere. We checked all the hallways," August says shakily, pointing at the three hallways branching off from the main one we are in. "It was all clear. And then he was just there. I don't even know how. He was just there, and he … and … he just … she's gone … " He breaks down into tears.

"Oh my goodness," whispers Carter, his face pale.

He checks Olive's pulse. "She's really dead … "

"You don't think I already checked her pulse?" snaps August, his eyes rimmed with red.

"What happened to the guard?" I ask.

"I-I killed him ... " August whispers, glancing to his left.

I now notice the limp body of the guard lying there.

"What else was I su—" August is cut off by Gia.

"No ... no ... please no ... " she says, as she sees Olive.

"She's gone, Gia," I murmur, my whole body shaking.

How did everything go so wrong? Why did I lead everyone into this mess?

I watch as Gia goes to check Olive's pulse.

"Hey, Carter and I both checked it. Don't you believe us?" says August angrily.

Gia ignores him. Artemis comes over to me and buries her head in my shoulder.

"We barely even knew her, Al. We'll never get a chance to now," she whispers.

I hug my little sister tightly, thinking about how quickly you can lose someone. Suddenly, a howling sound fills the air, and I nearly jump out of my skin.

"What was that?" I demand, my heart pounding.

Artemis whips out her wand, and the others pull out their weapons.

"Let's keep moving," I suggest.

"What do we do with Olive ... with her body?" Darren asks, his voice cracking. "I mean, she's ... gone. But we're not leaving her here."

"I-I don't know. But you're right. We can't just leave her here," I reply.

The howling noise comes again.

"I know what to do," Zoë says.

She shapeshifts into a small horse with amber fur. Carter seems to understand what she is trying to do, and lifts Olive onto Zoë's back.

Sweet, sweet Zoë. She is only six, seeing death close up, and yet she is still able to figure out what to do even when the rest of us can't.

"Okay. Onward," says August, attempting to keep his voice steady.

We spend a minute trying to figure out which of the three hallways to go down and eventually end up picking randomly. August walks next to me as we make our way down the dusty, damp hallway. Artemis walks next to me on the other side.

"So, I don't really know you that well, August. How old are

you?" I ask, trying to make conversation. Trying to keep my mind off of what just happened.

"17, almost 18. You?"

"14."

"I'm 10!" Artemis chimes in.

"When I was 10, I broke into the city bakery and stole baked goods for all the street kids," August says with a faint smile.

I can see Olive's death weighing on him, but I can tell he is trying to hide it. Her death hangs over the whole group like a storm cloud that won't go away.

"Did you know Olive well?" I ask quietly.

"We talked sometimes while we were in our cells. We weren't best friends or anything but... I mean she's dead. She's not coming back, Alavis," August replies, choking back tears.

"I know," I whisper, my voice trembling.

Darren drops back to walk with us. "You okay, Auggie?" Darren asks, his brow creased with worry.

I notice that August's face has gone deathly pale, his hazel eyes wide and unfocused. Darren gently puts his hand on August's shoulder. August flinches, tears starting to roll down his cheeks.

"What's going on?" I ask Darren.

"He has a bit of a traumatic past. His whole family was killed right in front of his eyes. He's usually able to hold it together, but sometimes he breaks down. And obviously seeing Olive die right before his eyes did not help," Darren explains.

"Will he be all right?" I ask worriedly.

"He'll be okay," Darren replies, his pale blue eyes filled with concern.

"Take a deep breath, Auggie. You're okay," Darren says to him.

August takes a deep breath, squeezing his eyes shut tightly. "S-sorry guys," he apologizes, opening his eyes back up.

"August, do you want to sit down for a minute?" I inquire.

"I'm fine," he replies quickly.

We walk in an awkward silence down the long hallway. How far away is this vault?

"So ... what powers did you use to have?" I ask, unsure of what to say.

August perks up a bit. "Electrokinesis, camouflage, and telekinesis," he says.

"Camouflage?" I repeat.

"Yup. I could blend in with my surroundings. It was awesome," he sighs.

Suddenly, there is a noise and my heart skips a beat.

"That was just my foot," August says.

"Oh."

I try to remember what we were talking about. "Well, you'll get your camouflage, and your other powers, back, August. You will."

"Olive won't," he mutters.

I stare at him, worried he will break down again.

"What powers do you have, Alavis?" asks August a moment later.

I sigh a breath of relief. "Fire, wind, invisibility, and telekinesis," I tell him.

"What about your sister?"

Before I can answer, Artemis interjects. "I'm Artemis. And I don't know any of my powers yet."

"What about the little red-headed girl?" August inquires.

"Zoë," I clarify.

"Yeah," August says.

"What about her?"

"She's young. And yet she has a power."

I glance over at Zoë. "Multiple, actually."

"Really? What else can she do?"

227

"Aside from shapeshifting, she has ice powers, teleportation, and invisibility. Oh and also this thing where she can make a magical figure that does what she wants," I inform him.

August looks at me questioningly. "So why doesn't she have the figure go kill Mailena?"

"Huh. I wonder if that would work. I think Mailena would just make it disappear. I bet she could do that, that awful, evil, horr—"

"Alavis, what are you doing?" August asks.

I look down and see that my hands and arms are covered in flames.

"Hey, it smells like smoke. What's going on?" Carter calls over his shoulder, a trace of worry in his tone.

He is walking with Gia in front of Zoë.

"All good! Alavis just thought it would be fun to have her arms go up in flames," Darren calls out.

August laughs, and I give them both a look. A moment later, Zoë neighs.

"She says she's tried to send her magical figure to get her parents back from the Marden, but it has never worked. So, she doubts it will work to send the figure to kill Mailena," Carter translates.

"How do you know that?" I demand.

"I-I don't know ... You couldn't tell what she was saying?" he asks confusedly.

I shake my head.

"New power, I guess," he shrugs, unexcited. "Don't see how talking to animals will help us though."

"I mean—" I start to say.

Gia suddenly interjects, fear in her voice. "Zoë, transform back. Now."

Zoë shrinks back into a little girl, and Gia catches Olive's body before it hits the floor. Now that there isn't a horse blocking my view, I see why Gia is scared. There is a metal door with a keypad, and guarding it is a pack of Alvasilvers.

Chapter 33

You know that one animal that everyone is always warned about? The animal that is murderous, malicious, and cannot be outrun? The one that, if you run into it, you're basically doomed? Well, those are the Alvasilvers. Three Alvasilvers step forward, their shaggy silver fur speckled with gold, and their long tails swishing against the floor. Sharp claws protrude from their paws, and their beady, knowing eyes lock with mine.

A deep, rumbling voice fills my head.

Alavis Hansen. The Alvasilver child. Did you know it is bad luck to be born in the Silver Month? We have a sixth sense, child. We always know what is going on with children born in the Silver Month. The month is, after all, named after us. Did you not know that? Yes, well, we knew you were coming. Olive Mackerson was also born in the Silver Month. We knew she was coming. We could always sense where she was. That is why she is dead. We sent that guard, child. We sent that guard to kill her.

"No. No, the curse of the Silver Month is just an old wives' tale. It isn't true. Sure, Alvasilvers are dangerous creatures, but they can't sense children born in the Silver Month. It's just a tale created to frighten children," I insist, my voice shaking.

"Alavis, who are you talking to?" Carter asks, his brow creasing with worry.

"You can't hear them?" I whisper.

"Hear who?" Zoë murmurs, her eyes wide.

Only children born in the Silver Month can hear us, the deep voice explains. *And it is not an old wives' tale, child. Our ancestor put a curse on that month, as revenge for the mass murder of his family. The curse protected the Alvasilvers, and punished the human race by cursing those born in the month of the murder.*

"But what did Olive do to deserve her fate?" I cry.

We killed Olive Mackerson because she knows the weakness of an Alvasilver. So she had to be gotten rid of. But that guard wasn't just supposed to kill her. He was supposed to kill all of you. Well, all except you, Alavis Hansen.

"Alavis, what's going on?" Darren asks.

His voice seems to come from faraway.

"They sent the guard to kill us," I whisper.

Yes, and he promised that he could kill as many as needed by himself. He has done it before, this guard. But he failed. He killed Olive Mackerson, but it appears the rest of you are still alive.

The deep voice fills my head with a tone of annoyance and disgust.

"Let us pass," Artemis demands.

We cannot do that. We have orders to kill anyone who tries to get the staff. Again, except for you, Alavis Hansen. You're quite the special girl. Queen Mailena wishes to kill you herself.

"What are they saying, Alavis?" asks Artemis, tugging at her knotty hair.

"They have orders to kill anyone who tries to get the staff," I explain, leaving out the part about Mailena wanting to kill me herself.

"Why haven't they killed us yet then?" inquires Darren.

The Alvasilver at the head of the pack tilts its head to the side scrutinizingly. *We are reasonable creatures. We wait to see what you have to offer. There is a chance you will be permitted to pass, depending on what you can give us in return.*

"They may let us pass, if we can offer them something they want," I say aloud, trying to stay calm.

Suddenly, I notice a faint whimpering sound. I spin around and see August crumple to the floor.

"August?!" I cry.

"He's unconscious!" shouts Gia.

"It's the Alvasilvers. They're the ones that killed his family," Darren tells us.

The head Alvasilver seems to be almost smiling, if an Alvasilver could smile, that is.

Ah, yes. We did kill the boy's family. Would you like to see, Alavis Hansen?

Suddenly, vivid images fill my head.

There is a little boy, no more than five years old, with shaggy blonde hair and wide hazel eyes. August. Next to him is an older girl, her expression terrified. In her arms is a wailing infant, and standing in front of the three of them are two people, who I assume are August's parents. And then I hear a low growl. A pack of Alvasilvers comes racing after August and his family.

"RUN!" August's mom shouts.

Her eyes, hazel like August's, are filled with fear. They all run as fast as they can, but the Alvasilvers are faster. Blood splatters onto the grass as August's mother and father are killed. August's older sister stops abruptly, frozen in shock, her golden hair speckled with blood.

"VANESSA, TILLY, NO!" August screams, as the Alvasilvers attack the girl and the baby in her arms.

August climbs up the nearest tree, as the Alvasilvers howl at the base. He shifts in the tree and something shiny tumbles to the ground. The Alvasilvers keep pacing back and forth near the tree. The scene replays over and over again.

"Stop it!" I shout at the Alvasilvers, but the scene keeps on playing. "STOP IT PLEASE!"

I hear continuous screaming, and at first I think it is just coming from August's family. Then, I realize it's also from me. I watch over and over as August's family is killed, and as young August climbs up the tree, his entire body shaking, sorrow in his eyes. I curl up in a ball on the floor, trying to get the images out of my head. If August is dealing with these memories all of the time... poor guy.

"Leave her alone!" shouts Artemis, pointing her wand at the head Alvasilver.

As Artemis is about to cast a spell, August regains consciousness, and takes in his surroundings.

"W-what's wrong with Alavis?" he asks.

Artemis replies, keeping her wand pointed at the Alvasilvers. "I don't know."

"What happened to bargaining with us?" says Gia.

We are ready to bargain, Alavis Hansen. We just wanted to show you what we can do. What we will do, unless you can give us a better offer than the Queen.

The scene of the murder of August's family vanishes. Shakily, I stand up. Artemis rushes over to me.

"Are you okay?" she asks anxiously.

"I'm fine," I reply, the image of the lifeless bodies of August's family lingering in my mind. I walk over to August, and give him a hug. "I'm so sorry," I whisper.

He seems to realize what the Alvasilvers showed me. "I'm sorry you had to see it."

Are you done? It's now or never, child. Do you have an offer? If not, it is time to kill your friends.

"No! We have an offer," I say quickly.

Everyone looks at me strangely. I realize how crazy I must look, talking to someone they can't hear.

"Um guys, what can we offer the Alvasilvers?" I ask.

"What the heck are we supposed to offer a bunch of hairy demons?" Darren scowls.

"This doesn't seem right," Gia says.

We all turn towards her.

"I've read plenty of things about Alvasilvers. They are many things, but reasonable is not one of them. I believe that they will kill us even after we give them something they want," she explains.

"I agree with Gia," Carter says.

"Maybe that's true, but what are we supposed to do? We need to get that staff," Artemis sighs.

All right, child. We have given you enough time. It is time to kill your friends, snarls the head Alvasilver.

"I'm so stupid!" I cry, an idea hitting me. I whip out my wand and murmur, "*Paralyze.*"

The Alvasilvers freeze in place.

"This probably won't hold them long. Start trying to get the door open," I order.

Everyone rushes toward the door. Carter stares at the keypad for a couple seconds, and then starts trying combinations. While he does that, I close my eyes, and think back to the scene the Alvasilvers showed me. There has to be some clue in there. What was that shiny object that fell to the ground? I replay the scene over and over in my head. Finally, I realize that it is a shiny blue pen falling out of August's pocket. And then, I notice a movement so slight that I would have never noticed it if I hadn't been specifically focusing on small details. When August's shiny blue pen hits the ground, the Alvasilver nearest it backs up the teensiest bit. As if the pen were poison or something.

"August, come here," I call out.

He runs over to me, almost tripping over the paralyzed Alvasilvers. "What's up?"

"When you were in the tree, the day your family was ... uh ... well you know ... a pen fell out of your pocket. The Alvasilver backed away from it. What was it?" I inquire.

"I'm trying so hard not to remember that day, Alavis," he whispers, his face pale.

"August, this could be their weakness. This could be how we defeat them and get to the staff," I reply. "If you really can't, I-I understand though."

"No, I'll try to remember," he sighs, closing his eyes. "It was shiny. It was ... bright blue, I think. It was made of some sort of gem. That's all I remember. I'm sorry, Alavis."

"Hey, Carter, do you know about any kind of shiny, bright blue gem?" I ask.

I remember him telling me once that he did a lot of reading back on Caldoria, so I figure he might have come across something about it. He pauses and thinks for a moment.

"Could be a couple things. Bluestone, Everleene, Kalleole, Delionan. Actually, Bluestone is more of a pale blue. I know that Everleene is only found on Camden. So it's probably either Kalleole or Delionan," Carter responds.

Darren pulls something out of his pocket with a mischievous grin. "Something like this?" he asks, holding up a sparkling, shiny blue watch.

Chapter 34

"What is that, and where did you get it?" asks August accusingly.

"I may or may not have taken it from the Princess' room," Darren shrugs. August sighs. "Darr—"

"Carter, keep working on getting the code," I interject, glancing anxiously at the paralyzed Alvasilvers who are just inches away from my feet.

With a nod, he turns back to the keypad.

"That could be it. We can try," I say to Darren hopefully.

Artemis laughs. "What are we going to do, throw it at the Alvasilvers?"

You will do no such thing, rumbles the head Alvasilver, the paralyzing spell worn off.

"Oh crap," I mutter.

And then, all hell breaks loose. The Alvasilvers charge, baring their sharp teeth. I surround my friends and I with fire, and the Alvasilvers growl, backing away from the bright orange flames. Darren and Artemis pull out their swords, and August unsheathes a dagger. I notice Zoë suddenly disappears. She reappears a moment later next to Darren, grabs the watch, and disappears again.

The fire starts to dwindle, every muscle in my body aching. Why does magic have to be so tiring? I watch as Zoë appears right next to one of the Alvasilvers and touches the watch to its shaggy fur. I hold my breath, praying that we have the right gem. For a moment, nothing happens. The Alvasilver lunges at Zoë, its eyes hungry and malicious. She thrusts out her hands, and the Alvasilver freezes, the room temperature dropping about 10 degrees. I glance over at Carter, and see two Alvasilvers moving over to where he is working to figure out the code. I glance back at Zoë.

"I'm fine. Go help him!" she says.

The last of my fire dies out, and I race over to Carter. The Alvasilvers attack, growling, and he floats upwards. They snarl, knowing he will have to come down eventually. With a blast of wind, I push the Alvasilvers backwards. Carter floats back down.

"Thanks," he smiles.

Internally, I am screaming, fighting the urge to blurt out how much I like him. But on the outside, I just shrug. "It was no big deal. You get the code yet?"

He doesn't answer, and I see why. The Alvasilvers are running forward again. Using my telekinesis, I lift them up into the air. Zoë appears out of thin air and gestures for me to lower the Alvasilvers down. I do, and she touches the watch to their fur.

"Zoë, I don't think we have the right gem," I tell her gently.

"Takes a minute," is all she says.

She disappears again, and I finally notice that a good portion of the Alvasilver pack are lying motionless on the floor.

"Are they dead?" I ask.

"I think they're asleep," Carter responds.

Then suddenly, he yells, "Zoë, no!" He points to one of the Alvasilvers lying on the floor near Zoë.

"What?!" Zoë cries.

"That one. It's faking! It's not really asleep!" he shouts.

A split second later, the Alvasilver jumps up and attacks Zoë. She falls over, the Alvasilver's sharp claws scratching at her skin. Her screams fill the air, and rage courses through me. Everything around me seems to disappear, and it's just me, Zoë, and the Alvasilver. I sprint toward Zoë, and, with my bare hands, I pull the Alvasilver off of her. Distantly, I am aware of all of the gashes and cuts I am getting in the process, but it doesn't matter to me. I need to help Zoë, who is now unconscious and therefore unable to defend herself. Lifting her up, I move her over to a new spot, away from the Alvasilver that attacked her. Out of the corner of my eye, I see the rest of the gang fighting the Alvasilver that I pulled off of Zoë, and a couple others that Zoë hadn't gotten to with her gem yet.

"Alavis, watch!" Carter yells, his voice faraway.

"Watch what?" I reply.

"No, I need the watch!" he clarifies.

Pulling it out of Zoë's limp hand, I toss it to him. I shake Zoë's shoulders.

"Please wake up, Zo. Please, I-I can't lose you," I whisper, holding her tiny hands in mine.

Her chest rises and then falls.

"Oh, thank goodness you're alive," I sob.

Her eyes slowly flutter open, and she squeezes my hand tightly. "That was scary. I didn't like being attacked by an Alvasilver."

"It's not a fun experience," I agree.

She glances at all of her cuts. "It hurts," she murmurs.

"I know, Zo. I know. You're going to be okay, I promise," I tell her.

"ALAVIS, MOVE!" shouts Gia suddenly.

I lift Zoë up and jump to the side, an Alvasilver landing in the spot where Zoë and I just were.

"That's the last one. We can do this," says Carter encouragingly.

"Alavis, you can hear them, correct?" Gia asks.

I nod, unsure where she is going with this.

"Distract the Alvasilver. I don't care how. Carter, sneak up on it," she orders quietly, so that the Alvasilver can't hear.

I nod again, and walk over to the creature. "Hello."

A high-pitched, scratchy voice responds in my head: *Shut up.*

"That's not very nice," I scold.

You're just trying to distract me, you irritating child. I won't let it happen. I am the Princess of the Alvasilvers, and you will show more respect.

"What's your name?" I inquire.

Maravella. But why do you care?

Carter starts to creep up behind Maravella.

"You know, have you ever thought about dying your fur? You could go for a nice fuchsia. Maybe yellow?" I say quickly.

Dying my fur? What is wrong with you, child?

"Nothing's wrong with me. But that's really not helping my self-esteem. So anyway, if you dyed your fur fuchsia, you would look really cool," I say, rambling on.

Carter is about to touch the watch to Maravella's fur, when she turns around.

You rotten child! I knew you were just trying to distract me!

Maravella attacks, teeth bared, and Carter jumps backwards, her teeth grazing his leg. He lets out a cry of pain and throws the watch to me, gesturing towards Maravella. I catch it as Carter floats upwards, sweating with the effort. Maravella growls and turns towards me. My heart pounding, I take a step backwards. My mind races, trying to think of an idea to defeat Maravella. And then, it hits me. I drop to the floor, faking a cry of pain. In my peripheral vision, I see my friends, their faces a mix of confusion and concern.

"Carter, code!" I call out, making my voice sound as pained as possible.

He hesitates, looking worried. Artemis locks eyes with me, and seems to realize almost instantly that I'm not actually hurt. She whispers something to Carter, and he breathes a sigh of relief, heading back over to the metal door to work on the code. Suddenly, I hear a deep growling noise and see Maravella making her way over to me, her eyes full of satisfaction. I resist the urge to smile. My plan is working.

Well, well, well. What's troubling you, child? Maravella says, her voice dripping with malice.

"It's my leg. It feels like it's being stabbed over and over again. I don't think I can move," I say, taking long and laborious breaths.

Maravella keeps moving until she is almost on top of me.

The Queen said she wishes to kill you herself. I'm afraid I'll have to disobey that order.

I clench the blue watch tightly in my sweaty palm, my heart racing. Maravella climbs on top of my chest, pausing a moment to revel in her victory. And just as I had hoped, she is letting her guard down, thinking she has already won. Quickly, I press the watch to her silvery fur and then try to push her off of me.

I hate you, Maravella growls in her annoying high-pitched voice.

She scratches at my face, and I scream, the pain and blood clouding my vision. I try to form a fireball, but I can't even muster enough energy to form a tiny spark. Every muscle in my body aches, and I feel like I have never been more tired in my life. I guess this is how I'm going to die. This is the end. And then suddenly, Maravella stops attacking me. Slowly, she curls up in a ball, and goes to sleep.

"It just takes a second," Zoë calls out.

"Yeah, I noticed," I reply.

And then I black out.

* * *

My eyes flutter open, and blurry faces swim in and out of my vision. A couple seconds later, their faces become clearer. Artemis and Gia stand over me, concerned looks on their faces. This picture is becoming a little too familiar. I really have to stop passing out.

I quickly take in my surroundings and see that Carter is still working on the code.

"You okay?" Artemis asks me, and I give her a look.

"Sorry. Stupid question," she says.

"I'll be fine," I sigh. "How long was I out?"

"About ten minutes."

"Guys, I figured out the code!" Carter shouts.

Gia reaches out her hand and helps me stand. I lean against her for support, and we walk over to the metal door, where Carter is standing. His eyes dance excitedly as he starts to pull open the door.

Then, he pauses and looks at me with a smile. "By the way, did I hear you tell that Alvasilver to dye its fur fuchsia?"

"Oh, shut up," I reply.

He laughs and turns back toward the door, pulling it the rest of the way open.

"What the heck?" mutters August, peering in.

"What?" I ask, taking a look myself.

The room is empty. Completely, utterly empty.

Chapter 35

"I-I don't understand. Where's the staff?" Darren asks, his eyebrows furrowed in confusion.

"How did we not realize?" mutters Gia.

"Realize what?" August inquires.

Gia sighs in frustration. "The Queen would not be stupid enough to just have the staff sitting here where anyone could take it. It's a staff full of tons of magic. If I were her, I wouldn't let it out of my sight."

I groan, angry that we fell for Mailena's tricks. "So she has it with her. I guess it's time for us to join the fight."

"But why did she send us down here? I don't understand," Darren says.

"There are three of us down here that have our magic. That makes us very powerful, no offense to the rest of you. So, Mailena must have thought that if she could just get us killed by the Alvasilvers, then she wouldn't have to deal with us and it would be easy for her to win," Carter ventures.

"That makes sense, but how did she know who would end up coming down here?" I ask, trying to fit the pieces of the puzzle together.

Carter shrugs. "Well, who told us the staff was down here? And that the most powerful should go?"

"Enna," I sigh. "I can't believe I actually trusted her."

"It was a mistake to trust her. A mistake that we all made, Alavis. But that's in the past, and now we need to go find the Queen and get that staff," Artemis says, and I take a deep breath before nodding in agreement.

"Okay, but what do we do with... Olive?" whispers August shakily.

I think for a moment. "We bring her with us I guess. We can

hide her body somewhere and then once we're done, assuming we survive, we can bury her. She deserves a proper funeral."

Gia lifts up Olive's limp body, and we head back the way we came.

* * *

After a little while of walking through damp, dimly lit basement hallways, we reach the staircase. We climb up about a million flights of stairs, and find ourselves back in the hallway, my eyes taking a moment to adjust to the brightness. The first thing we do is look for a storage closet to hide Olive in, everyone's cheeks wet with tears as we place her body down in the dark room.

Once we have done that, Carter asks, "So, where do we think Mailena is?"

"I'd say the fight might be the best place to look," sighs Gia.

"I agree," August says, his voice quiet.

I glance over at him and see that his eyes are full of sorrow, as are mine, and I'm sure everyone else's, too. I take a deep breath and push thoughts of Olive out of my mind. Right now, I need to focus on the task at hand.

"Well, then let's go find the fight," says Darren, giving us his signature grin. Only now, I can tell it is forced.

Suddenly, two teenagers, one a tall, thin girl with long, wavy red hair, and the other a boy with short, dirty blonde hair, come barreling down the hallway, three guards on their tail.

"I think the fight found us," I say.

"Remember the goal, everyone. Find Mailena, get the staff, give everyone back their magic," Carter reminds us.

"And what do we do then?" Artemis asks.

Carter shrugs with uncertainty. "I have no clue. We'll wing it."

The red-haired girl holds a bow and arrow and runs backward, shooting as she goes. She calls out to us, "Are you all just going to stand there, or are you going to help?"

I throw my hands out in front of me, but nothing happens. My head spins and black spots dance in and out of my vision. I guess I don't have the energy for any more magic right now. I glance at Zoë, who is clenching her teeth, trying to ignore the pain of a million cuts from an Alvasilver's claws. That's a feeling I can understand. The red-haired girl with the bow and arrow quickly pulls something out of her boot and throws it to me. I catch it and see that it is a tiny vial.

"Fatiga Juice. Stole a lot of it back on Caldoria," she explains.

I drink a little bit and then pass it around to the rest of the group. I feel energy start to return to my body, and I run over to help the girl. I throw my hands out in front of me, and this time a blast of fire comes out. The guards jump backward.

"I'm Teagan," says the girl, continuing to shoot arrow after arrow.

"Alavis."

"Cool name," she compliments.

"Thanks," I reply.

The blonde-haired boy, who is also shooting arrows at the guards, introduces himself. "I'm James."

"Nobody asked," Teagan snaps.

"Oh shut up, Teagan. You are the most annoying person that I have ever met and—"

"Hey, we're kind of in the middle of a fight," I remind them in exasperation.

Out of the corner of my eye, I see Artemis whip out her wand and whisper, "*Paralyze.*" The guards freeze.

"C'mon guys, let's go," she says.

We race down the hallway and eventually find ourselves in a huge ballroom, crystal chandeliers hanging from the ceiling.

Bouquets of wilted flowers sit all around the room, making me wonder how long it has been since this room was used. The room itself is filled with tons of people fighting. I scan the space looking for both the staff and JJ. Zoë tugs at my arm, and I follow her gaze across the room. JJ is trapped in the corner, a dagger against his throat. Zoë grabs my hand urgently, and we teleport over to him. I ignore the weird feeling teleporting gives my stomach, and with a strong gust of wind push the guard holding the dagger to JJ's throat to the ground. JJ quickly uses his ice powers to freeze the guard, and then he gives both Zoë and me a hug.

"JJ, it was all a trick. The staff isn't down there. We think Mailena has it," I explain.

"Well that sucks," he sighs. "I saw Mailena a little earlier. I think she's over there now."

He points across the room, and I see the evil queen herself standing on a raised platform, blasting people with all sorts of spells.

"I don't see a staff," Zoë notes.

I groan. "Me either."

"I'm sure if we ask Mailena nicely, she'll tell us where it is," JJ says sarcastically, and I roll my eyes.

"Should we teleport over to Mailena?" Zoë inquires.

JJ and I both nod. Zoë grabs our hands and we disappear. When we reappear by Mailena's platform, I feel like I'm going to throw up. I hate teleporting.

"Well, well, well, Alavis Hansen. We meet again," Mailena says with a creepy smile, turning her cold stare to me.

Chapter 36

M y blood turns to ice, and any bravery I was feeling before seeps quickly out of my body. "Where is the staff, Mailena?" I demand, my voice quivering.

"Are you really dumb enough to think I would tell you?" she laughs in response.

I clench my fists. "WHERE IS IT?" My whole body is shaking with fear and anger. "It's sad that you get so much pleasure from ruining the lives of innocent people. You left me and my sister orphans, and then you took her, the only loved one I had left, away from me! You are a psychopath if that makes you happy."

"Are you done with your dramatics?" snarls Mailena, pointing her wand at me. She starts to whisper something under her breath, and I quickly whip my wand out.

"*Protect*," I murmur, sweat dripping down my neck.

Nothing happens.

"I can't focus," I cry, my heart pounding like a stampede of wild animals.

"I'll handle it, don't worry," Zoë promises.

She disappears and then reappears right behind Mailena. The queen, however, is too busy focusing on casting a spell on me to notice the little red-haired girl crouched behind her. Mailena yelps in pain, dropping her wand in the process, as Zoë stabs her in the leg with a dagger.

"Go Zoë!" I exclaim, as she grabs the queen's wand and puts it in her pocket.

Mailena sighs, as if the dagger was nothing more than a pesky little needle. Reaching into her boot, she pulls out another wand, and points it at her wound, murmuring, "*heal*." The wound closes.

"Are you freaking kidding me?" JJ groans.

Zoë appears next to me again, and she and JJ both throw their hands out in front of them in an attempt to freeze Mailena. They are successful.

"I'd estimate we have only about 30 seconds. I've learned that the more powerful someone is, the shorter they stay frozen for," JJ tells us.

"We need a game plan. What do we do once she unfr—" I start to say.

"Hey, wait! Look!" interjects Zoë. She points to Mailena's frozen form. In her right hand is, what I assume to be, the staff.

"I don't understand. It wasn't there before," I say.

JJ thinks for a moment. "So she must have turned it invisible, but since the actual staff is still there, even if we can't see it, it froze."

Zoë takes a step forward, hesitates, and then continues to march forward, right over to Mailena. She reaches out her hand and tries to grab the staff. "OW!" Zoë shrieks.

JJ groans frustratedly. "Of course, there's some sort of protection spell."

"Hey, she's unfreezing," warns a vaguely familiar voice from behind me.

I glance over my shoulder and see Teagan standing there.

James joins her a second later.

"Thanks," I reply.

As Mailena thaws, I get my wand at the ready. Artemis does as well, and Teagan and James both draw their bows. All of a sudden, two guards come running at us, trying to distract our attention away from the queen. In a split second, Teagan and James have both fired their arrows at the guards' feet. The guards cry out in pain and hurriedly limp away.

"You guys have got skill," says JJ admiringly.

Teagan grins. "Why thank you."

"Yeah, thanks," adds James.

Then, I hear a blood-chilling laugh. "You really thought freezing me would do you any good?" Mailena chuckles, no longer a popsicle (sadly).

"Yeah, actually. It did do us some good," I snap.

There is a flash of uncertainty and worry on the queen's face, but it is gone a split second later. She gives an almost unnoticeable glance down to the area where the staff, now invisible again, was a moment before, and when she looks back at me, I can't tell if she knows that we have seen the staff or not.

"No matter. I am still more powerful than you, Alavis Hansen.

You cannot win," she booms, her voice dripping with arrogance.

I expect her to start casting a spell on me again, but she does nothing. She just stands there. Feeling a little confused, I use my telekinesis, pull the wand out of her hand, and throw it across the room. And yet, Mailena still seems unfazed. Teagan scowls, her brown eyes narrowed at the queen. My new friend nocks an arrow and shoots at the heart of the Queen of Elvaqua.

ChaptER 37

Everything seems to move in slow motion. The arrow whistles through the air, heading straight towards Mailena's heart. Mailena continues to stand in place, her face showing no sign of concern, even though she is wandless with an arrow flying at her. At the last second, the arrow diverts its path and comes sailing back toward Teagan. With a gust of wind, I push her out of the arrow's path.

"I don't understand. How ... " I trail off, speechless with surprise.

Teagan clenches her fists, her eyes blazing, and her cheeks flushed with fury. I have to say, I'm glad Teagan's on my side. She is not someone I would want to have as an enemy.

"Enna said she had seen her mother use the staff. Mailena must have gotten powers from the stolen magic," JJ says bitterly.

"DUCK!" screams Zoë, as electric sparks fly from Mailena's hands.

James yelps as one hits him in the arm. Teagan's face goes white, and she rushes over to make sure he's ok.

"Daughter," Mailena says suddenly, addressing the girl who has just appeared out of thin air next to her. The queen's tone is cold and angry.

Enna replies formally, "Mother."

"And what are you doing here? Did I not tell you to wait in your room until the fight was over?" Mailena snarls.

"I-I wanted to help you, Mother."

"You are just trying to win back my favor. You do not really wish to help. Dear child, do you really think that all is forgiven because you came back to my side? No, my daughter. You will not be forgiven for betraying your mother. For betraying your people. You will not be killed for your treason anymore because of your help in getting Alavis and her friends down in the basement with the Alvasilvers, and your warning of the fight that was to come. But you will not be the heir to my throne any longer. Unfortunately, Catalina cannot take over my throne when I pass on either, for she has also betrayed me by helping the prisoners get off of the planet. Luckily though, the guards managed to capture that blonde girl, even if all the others got away," the queen says, a twinkle in her eyes.

"Mother, I ... " Enna trails off, noticing JJ, who has gone still, his dark brown eyes wide.

"What did you just say?" he asks, his voice shaking.

Mailena smiles, clearly enjoying his pain. "I said that my guards captured that blonde girl. The one who came to the palace with you. She is somewhere now where you will never ever find her."

JJ drops to his knees, sobbing. "No ... NO!" he mumbles.

Mailena flicks her index finger, and sparks fly towards JJ. He doesn't notice. Zoë shrieks and grabs JJ's hand, both of them vanishing into thin air. Hopefully, they can get somewhere safe. I take a deep breath, an idea forming in my mind.

"Distract the queen and get her away from Enna," I whisper to Teagan.

She glances at the burn on James' arm worriedly.

"I'm fine, Teagan," he sighs, rolling his eyes.

"I don't care one bit if you're fine or not," she says quickly.

James smiles. "Yeah. Sure."

"We'll distract the queen, Alavis. Don't worry," Teagan tells me.

"Good. I need to have a little chat with Enna," I say.

"Hey, Mailena. So, good weather today, huh?" says Teagan, shooting arrow after arrow at the queen.

None of them hit her, but the constant need to flick away arrows to avoid being pierced with one keeps her attention away from Enna. I motion for Enna to follow me, and very reluctantly, she does. I push open the nearest door, which turns out to be a parlor, and the princess follows me in.

"What do you want?" she demands the moment the door shuts.

In less than a second, her wand is out and pointed at me. I quickly glance around the room to make sure we are alone.

"I just want to talk," I reply.

"Sure you do."

"First of all, what the hell happened? You were on our side. Remember that?" I snap.

Enna's cheeks color. "I didn't lie about being a rebellious

daughter. I've rebelled against my mom before ... but I've never done something that could get me sentenced to death. I committed treason, Alavis. That's unforgivable."

"But what changed? When did you turn against us?"

"Remember when we heard those footsteps, and I went out into the hallway to check who it was? And I told the guards that were out there to go to the dining hall? Well, that was true. But then, I ran into my mother. She promised me that if I helped her, my treason would be forgiven."

I give her a skeptical look. "And you believed her?"

"I think I knew, deep down, that treason would always be unforgivable in my mother's eyes. And I should have known that she wouldn't actually forgive me. But I let myself believe her despite all of that," Enna says.

"So you went back to her becau—"

Enna interjects. "That wasn't the only reason, Alavis. She just ... she reminded me how important family is. She's my mom, Alavis. I had to go back to her. Don't you understand?"

My blood boils. "No, you insensitive jerk, I don't understand. And do you want to know why I can't understand? Because your mother murdered my mom!" I shout, my body shaking with anger and exhaustion.

Enna sighs, disheartened. "I know. And I'm sorry, Alavis. Really, I am. But what do you want from me?"

I take a deep breath, trying to calm myself. "Do you know how to break the spell protecting the staff?" I inquire.

She crosses her arms over her chest. "I'm not telling you that."

"So you do know how," I infer.

Enna doesn't reply.

"Enna, listen to me. What do you think your future will be like in this palace? It's going to be miserable. You're not the heir to your mother's throne anymore. You will always be known as the girl who committed treason. If you tell me how to break the spell, you can come with us and get off of this planet," I beg.

She seems to consider this. "Why should I believe you? Why should I trust you?" Enna demands after a moment.

"I don't know what to tell you to make you trust me, Enna," I say with an exasperated sigh. "Do you really want to help your mother on this? She killed my friend Olive. She killed my parents. She imprisoned thousands of people—"

"That was the Marden. Not my mother," Enna interrupts.

"You're really telling me your mom has no connection to the Marden?" I say, raising my eyebrows.

"Well ... " Enna trails off.

"Yeah, that's what I thought," I mutter. "Look, Enna, your mom took people from the Marden, people who were imprisoned just because they have magic, which by the way, is something we don't even control because we're born with it! And then your mom drained them of their magic, which she had no right to do! Your mother has ruined so many lives, Enna. And she will continue to do so if you don't help me. Now, I need to get back out there and help my friends. You know what the right thing to do is." I start to leave.

"Alavis," she says.

I turn back around to face her and see that there are tears in her eyes.

"I don't know what to do, or who to be, anymore. I ... well ... " She pauses, and I wait for her to continue, the hope that she will join us filling my chest.

Enna takes a deep breath before talking again. "When you are raised by someone like Mailena, when she is your role model, you become a certain way. You snap at people and scream at them for no real reason. And I just blindly followed my mother for a while.

But when she killed my brother Edward, I couldn't just blindly follow anymore. That's easier said than done though. So, I rebelled in little ways. But this ... this treason ... this was not just a little rebellion. I went back to my mother because she promised she would forgive me and because she is my family. But also ... well I was scared, Alavis."

"It's okay to be scared sometimes, Enna," I assure her.

"I know. But ... I even thought that maybe I could change my mom. I thought I could make her be a better ruler and a better person. But, I don't think I can anymore. I want to help you. I'm just ... scared."

"It's really scary to take a stand. I know that. It's a big risk. But you need to decide: are you willing to take that risk, Enna?"

She pauses for a moment. "Yes."

I lock eyes with her. "Good. I'm glad."

"And once we defeat my mother, we can create this magical prison. I know how to. I read about it in a book once. And—"

"We need to get back out there. Tell me about it as we go."

Chapter 38

Enna and I rush out of the parlor, heading back towards Mailena. Before I can reach her, I see Carter, and my heart almost stops. He is lying on the ground, with a black eye, and a gash on his left leg. I kneel down next to him.

"Carter?" I cry. "Are you okay?"

"I'm fine," he assures me, his voice pained.

"You don't seem fine," I mutter.

"I'm fine, Alavis. I promise," he says. "Can you help me up?"

I extend my hand to him, and he takes it, wincing as he gets up.

"So, what's going on with the staff?" Carter asks, leaning against me for support.

"There's a protection spell around it. Enna's going to help us break it. And then, we're going to lock Mailena up in a magical prison," I say quickly.

Carter's face scrunches up in confusion. "I thought Enna wasn't on our side."

"She's helping us now," I explain.

Carter looks at me skeptically.

"Guys, there is a fight happening right now, in case you haven't noticed. The longer you stand there doing absolutely nothing, the more people that get hurt," Enna reminds us.

We make our way over to Mailena, and I try to ignore the growing exhaustion weighing me down. Teagan and James are shooting arrows at Mailena, along with a couple other people I don't recognize. I take a quick survey of the room and see Artemis heading over to me. I sigh with relief that she is still alive and well.

"There you are, Enna. Where have you been?" snaps Mailena when she notices her daughter standing next to me.

"Mother. Give them the staff. This is your last chance," Enna demands, her voice shaking.

"Excuse me?" the queen asks, as a guard comes up behind me.

I whirl around and try to push him backward with a gust of wind. But I can't. I'm too tired. The Fatiga is really catching up with me now. I stumble and then collapse on the floor, my heart pounding and my head spinning. The guard pulls out his knife, but before he can kill me, James glances over his shoulder and then shoots the guard in the leg. The guard howls in pain and drops to the ground.

"Thanks," I say gratefully, forcing myself to stand up.

James nods in response. I turn back towards Enna and the queen.

"Mother, I'm sorry. Truly, I am," says the former.

For the first time, I see fear in Mailena's eyes. Real fear. Enna points her wand at Mailena, murmuring a spell. The queen is unable to react fast enough, as she is busy avoiding being pierced by arrows. A loud shattering noise fills the room as the invisibility and protection spell around the staff break, and everyone freezes.

"Get the staff!" I shout.

Mailena clenches the staff tightly in her hand. "You will never get this staff," she growls.

"Yeah. Okay," says a voice.

I watch as Zoë appears out of thin air, grabs the staff, and disappears. Queen Mailena is frozen in shock as Zoë teleports throughout the room, touching the staff to people, giving them back their magic. The guards actually look kind of scared.

"Alavis, Artemis, take out your wands," commands Enna.

Mailena is starting to recover from her shock.

"You're going to repeat, *presone magicae evalei soramae*, five times," Enna whispers to us.

Then she shouts, "GUARDS! YOU KNOW WHAT THE RIGHT THING TO DO IS! HELP ME!"

To my surprise, some guards join us. We all point our wands at Mailena. A group of the prisoners we freed surround Mailena, holding daggers and swords. The queen seems to be forgetting that she has telekinesis and can make sparks fly out of her hands. She just stands there, an angry look on her face. Her eyes, however, are not angry. They are filled with terror.

"Do not listen to Princess Enna!" cries one guard.

This guard and some others start to attack. But many of us have our magic back now.

"We'll distract the guards. Do the spell," Teagan says.

She turns towards the guards, and something really strange happens. Some of them start to simply run away.

271

"I can amplify people's emotions. Like I can amplify their fear, for example," Teagan says when she sees my confused look.

"That's awesome," Carter says, nodding appreciatively.

"Okay, ready everyone?" Enna asks.

We start to chant, "PRESONE MAGICAE EVALEI SORAMAE! PRE—"

And just at that moment, Mailena comes to her senses. Sparks fly from her hands, and the people surrounding her drop their weapons as the sparks hit their hands.

"Stop at once, Enna," the queen booms.

"Never," Enna snarls. "KEEP GOING, EVERYONE!"

We continue to chant, Enna's voice the loudest of us all. More and more guards join us.

"PRESONE MAGICAE EVALEI SORAMAE! PRESONE MAGICAE EVALEI SORAMAE! PRESONE MAGICAE EVALEI SORAMAE!"

"Guards, stop them!" screams Mailena.

Some of her guards do try to stop us. But they are pushed back by everyone we rescued from the cells, with their newly returned magic.

"LAST ONE! COME ON EVERYONE!" cries Enna.

The room is filled with the glow of the wands casting the spell.

"PRESONE MAGICAE EVALEI SORAM—"

We are cut off this time by Mailena using her telekinesis to lift daggers off the floor and throw them at us. But before they can hit us, they are stopped by a forcefield suddenly surrounding us.

"Man, it feels good to have my magic back," grins Darren, his eyes twinkling.

Chapter 39

"**B**reak the forcefield when I say, 'now'," Enna orders. Darren frowns, his shaggy auburn hair falling into his eyes. "No thank you?"

"Fine. Thank you. Now, when you break it, we just have to finish the last word of the spell, and then my mother will be forever locked up in a magical prison," explains Enna.

I can tell that despite everything, it pains her to do this to her mother.

"What about the guards still loyal to her?" I inquire.

Enna shrugs. "We'll cross that bridge when we come to it."

She stares at her mother, waiting for her to glance away from us. A few seconds later, the moment comes. Mailena turns around to fight off Teagan and James who have run up behind her.

"NOW!" shouts Enna.

The forcefield shatters.

"SORAMAE!"

The spell is finished. As shimmering purple walls start to close around Mailena, she picks a dagger up off of the floor. With all her might, she hurls it at me. But her aim is off. I watch in horror, frozen in place, as the dagger slices through the air, burying itself in Enna's heart.

"NO!" Mailena cries. "ENNA! NO! I'm so sorry, my daughter. I-I love you, Enna. I'm sorry. I—" The queen breaks off sobbing in despair, and then the walls have completely closed, and we cannot see her anymore. The magical prison we have created disappears into thin air, with Queen Mailena inside.

I kneel down next to Enna. "I'm so sorry, Enna," I murmur.

"It's not your fault," she whispers, her face turning pale. Then she smiles. "My mother said she loves me. She's never said that before."

"Oh, Enna. You are such an amazing person. We could not have done this without you. Thank you so much," I tell her, fighting back tears.

"Alavis is right. We couldn't have succeeded without you," Carter adds.

Enna smiles again, her breathing becoming more and more labored. "Alavis?"

"Yeah?"

"If for some reason you need to get the prison back, you just repeat the spell backward," she tells me. "And ... the book ... mother's desk ... will help you find your friend ... "

"Thank you. I'll remember that. And, Enna, we will always remember you," I promise her, tears rolling down my cheeks.

"That means so much to me," Enna whispers.

I take her hand in mine, watching as the life leaves her eyes.

Chapter 40

A few moments later, Enna is gone, and I stand up shakily. I find Artemis, who wraps me in a tight hug.

"I couldn't save her," I mumble.

"It wasn't your fault, Al," Artemis promises.

"But it was my fault. I should have done something. I should have stopped it."

Artemis shakes her head. "Alavis, listen to me. You can't save everyone. You just can't."

I take a deep breath. "I wish I could."

"I know. Me too, Al. Me too."

Darren clears his throat awkwardly. "Al, um, we have some stuff to deal with."

Artemis and I glance around the room. Most of the guards are milling about, uncertain of what to do. There are a few, however, that are still fighting.

"For the Queen!" shouts one, attempting to stab Teagan.

She dodges the blade easily.

"The Queen is gone. There is no reason to continue to be loyal to her," argues another guard, knocking the blade out of his fellow guard's hand.

I watch as one of the guards, a woman with curly brown hair and a fierce look in her eyes, gets up on the platform Mailena was on earlier. "Fellow guards!" she calls out, her voice clear and strong.

The fighting pauses, and everyone turns to face her.

"Queen Mailena murdered her own daughter. She also murdered her own son, or have you all forgotten about Edward? Tell me, is this the kind of leader you want to be supporting?" she asks.

"Both of those murders were an accident, Quinn!" shouts the guard who tried to stab Teagan.

The woman on the platform, who I assume must be Quinn,

sighs with exasperation. "Queen Mailena has done many horrible things in her life. She is gone, and she is not coming back. Why would you continue to support her? She has killed so many people and ruined so many lives. And, guards, has she ever treated us well?" The room is silent for a minute, and then Quinn speaks again. "So, does anyone still need me to change their minds?"

Nobody responds.

"Good," says Quinn, stepping down from the platform.

She walks over to me and holds out her hand. "Quinn Rileigh," she introduces herself.

I shake her hand. "Alavis Hansen."

"Well, Alavis, what's the plan now?" Quinn inquires.

I think for a moment, as everyone begins to gather around us.

"We need to create some sort of new ruling system for Elvaqua," I say.

"And free the people in the Mardens on Caldoria, Zathen, and Denima," Carter adds.

JJ walks into the room, his cheeks wet with tears. "And we need to find Talia." He sees Enna, and his face goes pale. "What happened?"

"Mailena tried to kill me, but she killed Enna instead," I say, my voice trembling.

"Mailena killed her own daughter?" he replies, his eyes wide with shock and sadness.

I nod.

"That's ... that's awful," JJ murmurs.

Suddenly, I remember something Enna said to me as she was dying.

"JJ, Enna told me that there is a book on her mother's desk that will help us find Talia," I tell him.

Taking a shaky breath, he says, "I'll be back." He leaves the room again, in search of the book.

Meanwhile, I look around for Gia.

"Gia!" I call out when I spot her.

She comes over to me. "Yes?"

"Um, what happens to the Elvaquins now?" I ask.

Gia is the wisest person I know. She'll know what to do ... hopefully.

"What do you mean?" Gia inquires.

"Well, shouldn't we be helping them pick a new leader or something? Maybe create a new system of government? Just kind of help them get things in order?" I explain.

"Hmm. A team of us could stay to help, yes. I can be one of them, and I'll go find some more right now. I don't really think everyone needs to stay though," Gia suggests.

"But ... that doesn't seem fair. Don't you want to go home?" I say.

She shrugs. "Where? Caldoria was my home. What is there for me to go back to on Caldoria? I have no desire to return there."

"But what about Masthinya? You could go there," I offer.

"Alavis, someone has to do this. I don't mind. Really, I don't. Now, I'm going to find some others who will stay here with me." She walks away.

"What's next?" asks a voice from behind me.

I whirl around.

"Sorry, I didn't mean to scare you," Carter says apologetically.

"You didn't."

"Okay. I was just wondering what else we need to do before we can leave," he explains.

"Well, JJ's finding the book, and Gia and some others will stay here to help the Elvaquins get things in order. I guess all that's left is getting everyone on the ships," I tell him.

Carter nods. "Alright. I'll go find where the ships are being held, and then we can start loading everyone on."

He runs off, and I turn toward Enna's body, my heart heavy. August is kneeling next to her.

"Hi, August."

"Hi Alavis," he replies quietly.

"Are you okay?" I ask.

He shakes his head. "How could I be? How could anyone be, if someone is dead?"

"That's a good point. I just meant ... I was just checking up on you," I say gently.

Suddenly, I hear a series of loud crashes. Instinctively, flames sputter to life in my palms, and I look around for the source of the sound. A few minutes go by, and then JJ comes limping back into the room, holding a big, dusty book.

"I heard a crash. Is everything okay?" I inquire, noticing blood dripping from a gash on his cheek.

"I'm fine," he says. "I should have known I wouldn't just be able to walk up to the desk and grab the book."

"What happened?" I ask.

He wipes away some of the blood. "I'm fine."

"That doesn't answer my question, JJ." I feel myself starting to get upset. "Why won't you tell—" I pause, and take a deep breath. If he doesn't want to tell me, I'm sure there's a reason. But it's nothing to get angry over. I take a few more deep breaths. Nothing to get angry over.

"Look, Alav—" JJ starts to say, but he is cut off by Carter returning from his search for the spaceships.

"Alavis, I found the ships!"

"Good. But, who's going to pilot them? You can't fly multiple ships at once, Carter," I remind him.

"I have a plan. Zoë?" Carter calls out.

She appears next to him, her body sagging with exhaustion. "What?"

"Can you make us some magical pilots?"

She smiles. "It would be my pleasure."

"Wait!" I cry.

"What?" Zoë asks.

"Olive."

Carter realizes what I mean, rushes off, and returns with her body.

"We can properly bury her, Enna, and any others who died when we get to Masthinya," I say, somberly.

Then, Carter leads us all out of the palace and to a giant field with hundreds of spaceships. We begin to board, bringing the bodies of the dead with us.

Chapter 41

We've been on the ship for a few weeks now, and I think we're supposed to be landing on Masthinya today. My heart races with excitement, and I can barely eat my breakfast. Not that spaceship food is any good anyway.

"Hey Al," says Teagan, sitting down next to me.

I grin. "Hi. I can't believe we're landing today."

"Same. I've never been to Masthinya before. Is it nice?" she asks, and I nod in response.

"Alavis!" Zoë calls out from the other room.

"What?"

"Can you braid my hair?" she asks.

I laugh. "Sure."

Teagan and I head out into the sitting area where Zoë is. She sits on my lap.

"Two braids please," she says.

As I am braiding her wild red curls, James walks into the room, his blonde hair neatly combed.

"Hi, Teagan. Hi, Alavis. Hi, Zoë," he greets us.

Then, he goes into the kitchen to eat breakfast. I look over at Teagan, whose cheeks are pink.

"Looks like someone's got a little crush," I tease.

"I do not! And if we're going to talk about crushes ... " She grins at me.

"Oh be quiet," I frown.

"Are you talking about how Alavis likes Carter?" Zoë asks, feigning innocence.

"Zoë, you do want me to braid your hair, don't you?"

"Yes, yes. Forget I said anything," she says, her eyes twinkling with amusement.

As if on cue, Carter comes into the room. "Alavis, can I talk to you?"

Teagan and Zoë exchange a look.

"Sure. I'll finish your hair later, Zo, okay?" I say.

She nods. "Okay."

I get up and follow Carter into the hallway.

"There's something I've been wanting to tell you. And, I know that you may not feel the same way bu—"

"Guys, we're here!" interrupts Darren, racing past us.

I glance at Carter, and then back at Darren. My excitement that we have arrived overpowers my curiosity at what Carter was about to tell me, and I follow Darren, my heart pounding. He opens the doors of the ship, and we all step out. Just like when I first arrived on Masthinya, Brightstar is setting over luscious green hills, and the beauty of it takes my breath away.

"It's amazing," Teagan murmurs.

August nods in agreement. "It really is."

"We should move. There's another ship coming in," Carter suggests, glancing at me.

I wonder what he was going to tell me. I'll probably find out later. For now, I push it out of my mind.

"Hold hands, everyone," orders Zoë. "To Joy's house?"

"To Joy's house," I reply excitedly.

Darren looks at me. "Wait, how will everyone else know where to go?"

"Zoë and James are going to come back and teleport people there," I remind him.

Apparently, James also has the power to teleport.

"Oh, right," Darren says. "I knew that."

We all hold hands, and the world around us disappears. For a moment, everything is dark and eerily quiet, and then we are outside of Joy's house, with birds chirping and the sound of the grass squishing beneath our feet. It takes a moment before the nauseous feeling in my stomach goes away, and then the front door swings open. Joy rushes out, a hooded coat covering her dark purple curls.

"You're back! Did you find your sister?" she exclaims.

I nod as Artemis steps forward.

Joy smiles. "Oh, that's wonderful!"

"And we have the stolen magic. So everyone can get their powers back," I add.

"Everyone will be so happy to hear that. I'll let the people know right away. And, you all are welcome to stay at my house. I have tons of room," Joy says.

"There are going to be a lot more people coming, Joy. We found out that the Queen of Elvaqua had been bringing people from the Marden to Elvaqua to take their magic. We freed all of the prisoners," I tell her.

"Well, I will spread all of this news to everyone in town. I'm sure people would be willing to give out spare rooms. Oh, and feel free to head on inside. The door is unlocked." Then, she rushes off excitedly.

Everyone, except Zoë and James, goes inside and sits down in the living room. I glance over at JJ, whose nose is already in the book from Elvaqua. While it is nice that we are here on Masthinya, I know that I will be leaving again very soon, as will many others. Once JJ can figure out where Talia is, he'll set off to find her. And some of us will have to deal with the Mardens. We will have to free all of those prisoners. But for now, I'll try to relax.

ChaptER 42

I wake up the next morning to the sounds of a screaming match. How lovely. I storm down the stairs, and see Teagan and James standing in the kitchen, glaring at each other.

"YOU ARE THE MOST ANNOYING PERSON EVER! THAT WAS MY MUFFIN, AND YOU STOLE IT!" shouts Teagan.

James shouts back, "NO, IT WAS MY MUFFIN, AND YOU STOLE IT!"

"You're joking, right?" I mutter.

Teagan scowls. "This is no joking matter, Alavis."

"Yeah, okay," I reply, heading back upstairs.

I guess since I'm up, I might as well start getting ready. I brush my hair out in the mirror and then open the closet door. The long black dress Joy gave me last night is hanging there, and I put it on. Today, we are having a burial for all of those who died: Enna, Olive, and eight others that we know of. I lie down on my bed again, closing my eyes in an attempt to try and push away the images of Enna's lifeless eyes, Olive's limp body, and the murder of August's family. Those images will forever haunt me.

* * *

"Alavis! It's time to go!" yells Artemis, jolting me awake.

"You fell asleep," she informs me.

"Good observation," I reply.

She squeezes my hand, and we walk downstairs, and then out the front door. A large procession of people make their way to a field a couple miles in the distance. When we get there, I see a beautiful yellow flower just beginning to bloom. It breaks my heart. How can something that beautiful exist when my friends have died? I watch as ten coffins start to be lowered into holes in the ground. Artemis buries her face in my shoulder, her tears wetting my dress.

A woman I don't recognize steps forward, with sharp features and long brown hair. "Today, we say our final goodbye to ten people. They were killed on Elvaqua. There may be others that were killed on Elvaqua that we do not know about. May all these brave souls rest in peace," she booms.

I watch as the coffins are covered with dirt, and then they disappear from sight.

"Goodbye Enna. Goodbye Olive," I murmur.

I didn't even really know Enna and Olive that well, but their deaths make me feel as if a piece of myself is missing. A piece that I can never get back.

* * *

It is about five hours after the burial, and I am sitting inside a big town hall building. Everyone is here to get their magic back. Joy has the staff in the front of the room, and everyone else has been given numbers. There is a buffet, and people are sitting at tables, eating while they wait for their number to be called.

"27!" calls Joy.

A woman walks up to the front excitedly. I, however, am far from excited. I am engulfed in sadness for Enna, Olive and those eight others who died. The hall starts to feel very claustrophobic, and I head outside, breathing in the fresh air. There is a little gazebo with lights strung around it and a wooden bench. Taking a seat, I try to forget about my sadness for a moment.

"Alavis!" Carter shouts, walking out of the hall and in my direction.

"Hey. What's up?" I reply.

"I never got to finish telling you what I was trying to tell you on the ship," he explains.

"Oh. Go ahead," I say.

He runs his fingers through his hair nervously. "Well. You see … now, I know you probably don't feel the same way … but I just … I have to tell you. I … I like you, Alavis … and not just as a friend."

Butterflies start dancing around in my stomach, and my brain just keeps saying over and over:

HE LIKES ME, HE LIKES ME, HE LIKES ME

I can't seem to form the words to respond to him.

"Okay … well … I'll go. Um, I guess you don't feel the same way … it's fine, really," Carter says, his cheeks bright red.

He starts to walk away.

"Carter, wait!" I cry.

He turns back around, his eyes hopeful.

"I-I like you, too. And not just as a friend," I tell him.

Carter walks back toward me and sits down. "Really?" he asks.

"Really."

There is an awkward silence for a moment.

"What happens now?" I say.

Carter hesitates for a second and then leans in and kisses me. The butterflies in my stomach go crazy.

"I've been wanting to do that for a while," he says. "You know, I've had a crush on you since the moment I met you."

"Aw, you have?" I smile.

His cheeks turn red again. "Yeah."

"I've had a crush on you since the moment I met you, too," I tell him.

"Do ... do you want to go on a date? We can go somewhere in town tomorrow night. Unless you're busy," Carter asks.

"Oh, gee, let me check my schedule," I say sarcastically.

He punches me playfully on the shoulder.

I laugh. "Carter, what would I be busy doing?"

"I don't know!" he replies.

"Well, I'm not busy, and I'd love to go on a date with you tomorrow night," I say.

Suddenly, I hear a voice calling my name. It's Artemis' voice. She might be in trouble.

"I have to go," I tell him, rushing off.

I push open the door to the town hall and see Artemis pacing back and forth excitedly.

"Alavis, I got my first power!" she squeals. She walks over to a long wooden table, and picks it up with one hand. Then, in her other hand, she picks up another table.

"Super strength!" I exclaim. "How did you discover that?"

"One of the tables fell over, and it fell on this little kid. I knew I had to help him, so I picked up the table with one hand and picked him up with the other. I don't know how. I just did," she explains.

I hug her. "I'm so proud of you, Artemis."

"Thanks. I'm proud of me, too," she grins. "Alavis, you look very happy. Did something happen?"

"You got your first power," I remind her.

She shakes her head. "I don't think that's the whole cause of your happiness ... "

"Well, if you must know, Carter kissed me," I say quietly.

"He did?!" Artemis exclaims.

Teagan squeals, overhearing me. "HE DID?!"

"Yes, he did," I reply, motioning for them to be quieter.

"I knew this would happen. I just knew it!" says Teagan.

"And, we're going on a date tomorrow night," I add.

"I'm helping you pick out an outfit," Teagan insists.

"Me too," says Artemis.

I laugh. "Okay, okay, you can both help me!"

"This is so exciting!" grins Teagan.

Though I know it probably won't last, I feel happier and calmer than I have felt in a very long time.

* * *

That night, as I'm lying in bed, Artemis' voice echoes in the darkness.

"Alavis?" she whispers.

"Yeah?"

"Do you think mom and dad would be proud of us?" she asks.

I smile. "Yeah, I think they would be."

About the Author

Sabrina Grossman is 15 years old, and has loved writing from the time she was little. Aside from writing, she loves theater, singing, reading, and hanging out with her friends and family. She lives in New York with her mom, dad, older sister Maya, and her two cats Midnight and Shadow.

CPSIA information can be obtained
at www.ICGtesting.com
Printed in the USA
LVHW051134080722
723039LV00008B/527